John Hyde is a 38-year-old writer and former broadcaster. After leaving school at the age of fifteen, he travelled extensively throughout Europe before settling in Canada where he held a variety of jobs from working in a gold mine to driving a truck for a circus. He then joined a newspaper and by his own admission learnt his trade the hard way before rising to the editorship of a monthly magazine. He also hosted his own radio and television shows before returning to England.

He now lives in Sussex with his wife. *Amen* is his second novel; his first was *The Prediction*, which was received with enthusiasm and acclaim on both sides of the Atlantic. He is currently at work [illegible] o be published ne[illegible]

This is for my mother, Mary,
who probably wishes it wasn't!
And for Katie who still sees
dark shadows in the night!

John Hyde

Amen

Futura
Macdonald & Co
London & Sydney

A Futura Book

First published in Great Britain by
Macdonald & Co. Publishers Ltd.

ISBN 0 7088 2105 7

Filmset, printed and bound in Great Britain by
Hazell Watson & Viney Ltd, Aylesbury, Bucks

Futura Publications
A Division of
Macdonald & Co. (Publishers) Ltd
Holywell House
Worship Street
London EC2A 2EN

Unstoppable, his hand was compelled to his own throat, the finely honed blade-edge pressing into his Adam's apple. The force held it there while the entity exhorted Falangi to draw the blade across the throat himself.

He felt the strength draining from him as he stood there in the macabre tableau. He was so tired of it all and so longed for a rest from the evil beings which tormented his body and soul. Perhaps it wouldn't be so bad to end it. Who could blame the man for not having the strength to withstand more pressures in two years than a thousand others would face in a thousand lifetimes?

The author gratefully acknowledges the help and assistance given to him by Mr Martin Whalley during the researching and writing of this novel.

PROLOGUE

1956, Newark, New Jersey

The music from the small four-piece band wafted over the dancers and the strains of a current pop tune were hummed by the waiters as they darted between tables with their overburdened trays.

For Mary and Michael Downing this night was special in more ways than one. It was the first night they had been able to be alone for six months, thanks to Michael's insistence that the baby was too young to be left with a sitter; it was also their wedding anniversary and Mary's birthday.

Mary drummed her fingers on the crisp white tablecloth, her face alight with the pleasure she felt at escaping from the house for a few short hours. She loved her husband and the baby of course, but lately she thought she would go mad with the seemingly never-ending household chores. The beautiful house, bought three weeks after their wedding with a loan from a favourite uncle, had started to seem like a prison. Her mother had said it wasn't natural to want to leave a young baby, not even for just a few hours, but Mary knew that this one very special night was just what she needed to break the monotony of her existence. And Michael had agreed the baby was now old enough to be left with a capable baby-sitter.

The music stopped and the musicians stepped down from their platform. An unseen hand flipped a switch and canned music filled the room. It was important the ambience be maintained.

'Happy?'

Mary smiled up at her husband. She was very proud of him. At six foot three and seemingly just as broad she still got a thrill watching other women turn their heads at her handsome man. They had been fortunate to come out of the war as a whole, she knew that. Michael had been badly injured in 1944 while leading his platoon on an assault on some obscure Pacific island. Twelve months of hospital treatment had left him with an almost imperceptible limp, a Purple Heart and a discharge from the army. The rest of the war had been spent working in his father's small radio station, an occupation he had enjoyed and one which he felt, and had since proved, could give them a comfortable living.

'Very happy, darling, and very relaxed. Thank you.'

'What for?' he laughed lightly and easily through the question and Mary beamed.

'For understanding that I needed this break. I know you hate leaving the baby, and I do too. But it is important for us to have time on our own – like this, when we can just be with each other without cocking one ear all the time in case the baby wakes up.'

Michael reached across the table and clasped her hand. 'I know, honey, and I guess I've been stupid about it. It's just that my mother and father always went out and left me with sitters. I grew up in a house where my parents didn't care enough, or at least so it seemed to us kids, to stay in and look after us. I don't ever want Gemma to feel that terrible fright and loneliness.'

She squeezed his hand and out of the corner of her eye spotted the band returning to the stage. 'Well, I'll call home just to make sure the sitter hasn't set fire to the place and then we'll have a few dances. That's if you can still remember how to!'

He grinned at her as she stood up from the table. 'You bet your life I remember.'

Michael's eyes followed her as she walked towards the powder room and he saw a still curvaceous and trim thirty year old. They had met in college like millions of other couples and theirs had been the Hollywood love story. Michael was the star quarterback and Mary the prettiest cheerleader on campus. But from the start there was more that bound them than purely physical attraction. Both had a deep passion for English literature and it was this mutual love which took them beyond the hasty coupling in the back seat of his '42 Chevy to a more permanent relationship. He had been deeply impressed with her grasp and understanding of politics and current affairs and she, in turn, had been inspired by his deep conviction about the civil rights of minorities. It was only after they had married that she confessed that joining the cheerleader squad had been a ploy to get closer to him and attract his attention.

As he watched her thread her way back through the tables, he thought about how deeply he loved her and how lucky he was that she had come along. He also thanked God that his life hadn't been snuffed out by the three Japanese bullets which had torn their way through his body.

'Everything O.K.?'

She frowned. 'Caroline said it was . . .'

'But?'

'I don't know. The radiogram was playing pretty loudly. Michael, do you think she's having a party at our house? You know you hear such stories about baby-sitters having boys around to houses while parents go out. I'm worried, Michael!'

He took her hand in his again to give it a reassuring squeeze and he was alarmed to feel it trembling. 'Honey, it's natural for kids to play music loudly; I'm sure there's nothing to worry about. The orphanage allows only the most sensible girls to baby-sit for extra money. They vet them very carefully, teaching them first aid and baby care. You know that, so stop worrying. It's natural for you to be concerned, particularly as this is the first time we've left Gemma with a stranger. Now come on, let's dance!'

He stood up, tugging gently on her hand. She rose reluctantly, allowing him to lead her towards the postage stamp of a dance floor. Suddenly she stopped and pulled him back. 'I've just remembered. Caroline said she was roasting a chicken for supper.'

'So? We said she could cook something if she got hungry.'

She turned on her heels, walked back to the table and picked up the small gold lamé purse which Michael had bought for her birthday and clutched it determinedly. 'That's just the point, Michael, we haven't any chicken in the freezer. Someone has taken a chicken over to the house. I'm sure she has boys round which means she can't be listening out for the baby. I want to go home!'

Michael looked at her for a long moment feeling both anger that Mary could be so possessive of the child after all the pleading for a night out and concern that she just might be right. He waved over their waiter, quickly peeling off four fives from his billfold before hurrying through the restaurant and into the parking lot.

In the cooler air he felt again the anger at a ruined evening and remarked that they were going to look very foolish if, on arriving home so obviously early, everything was as it should be. Mary sat mute in the Pontiac, afraid to answer in case it sparked off another row.

As they entered the familiarity of their neighbourhood

she felt increasingly apprehensive. Carefully vet the girls the orphanage might do, but Mary understood that in such a restrictive place as St Angela's Orphanage it would be quite natural for a young girl to seize any opportunity to meet with a boy. Baby-sitting jobs were perfect for such assignations.

Michael slipped the key into the latch and, as the solid front door swung open, the loud radiogram finished proclaiming Eddie Fisher's love. There was nobody in the lounge, which was as neat and tidy as they had left it; everything seemed normal. Michael moved towards the kitchen from where he could hear faint humming from the girl as she replayed the strains of the song over in her head. Mary ran quickly up the stairs to check on Gemma in the nursery at the far end of the landing.

Caroline wheeled around as Michael pushed open the kitchen door. 'Hello, Mr Downing, you're back early.'

Michael smiled at the implied question. 'Headache,' he mumbled, hoping the girl wouldn't press any further. He felt foolish at their sudden arrival now that he was standing in the warm kitchen with the reassuring smell of cooking food assailing his nostrils. He thought suddenly of the main course which they hadn't had time to eat at the restaurant and he felt annoyance again at his wife's needless concern.

'Smells good, Caroline,' he said conversationally, the aroma drawing him towards the oven.

As he peered through the glass Mary burst through the kitchen door, her eyes wide in panic. 'Gemma's not in her cot!' she screamed.

Time froze for Mary as she waited for either Michael or Caroline to answer. Didn't they understand the baby wasn't there? She looked towards Caroline, who retreated a little, a bewildered expression on her face. Mary felt surging panic as she turned to Michael for an explanation.

Michael stepped back from the oven, his face ashen. He staggered backwards until the edge of the work surface smashed into his spine, the pain unfelt. His hands flew to his mouth and suddenly he turned, vomiting into the sink.

Mary hesitated slightly before going to him, concern for him mingling with her fear for her baby.

She touched his arm and he turned to look at her, pain and horror written deep into his handsome face. She turned slowly and looked towards the oven, trying to trace the cause of his horror. There was nothing to see. After a long moment she stepped across the kitchen and peered into the dimly lit oven.

At first Mary's mind couldn't comprehend what she saw. Then, slowly, as the dark veil lifted from her she started to scream at the sight of her baby gently revolving on the rotisserie.

CHAPTER ONE

1979, County Roscommon, Eire

The small saloon car sped rapidly along the winding country road, skirting skilfully the stagnant puddles of rain which had collected the night before, the result of a torrential downpour which had lasted for several hours, threatening to burst the banks of the River Moy as it wound its way south to Kilmore.

The plainclothes security officer swung the wheel hard left to avoid a loaded wagon which had suddenly meandered out of a field and grunted an apology to the two men in the back of the car before returning his attention to driving along the unfamiliar and, as he had just discovered, potentially dangerous back roads of the Republic. The officer swore softly to himself at the thought of the accident he had avoided by inches and cursed the dim-witted farm labourer. He glanced into the rearview mirror and shuddered as he thought what his superiors would have said if either of his two passengers had been injured. Or worse, killed! He swore again, an oath which would have shamed a docker, and then hurriedly muttered a penance as he glanced again in the mirror and saw the deep blue eyes studying him with a slight hint of amusement. It was almost as though this man knew what he was thinking!

They swung around Charlestown, avoiding the town in case an alert local recognised the passengers, and rejoined the third-class road which ran north.

Suddenly, the driver's blue-eyed passenger indicated

excitedly to his companion and both craned their necks to stare out of the half-curtained rear window at something the driver himself had missed. That bothered him because he should have been aware of everything, *everything*, along their route in case Provos had got wind of this unscheduled journey.

O'Casey wasn't the sort to worry unduly about extremists of any persuasion but he was a realist and could still feel the cold sweat of horror which had covered him when he was informed that the two men wanted to be taken to Dragha Abbey – and worse, that they were to travel in an unmarked car with only himself as security.

Side trips on official visits were quite normal. He had experienced many unscheduled trips with various VIPs and assorted heads of state to an equally assorted number of destinations. Most of them the sort that the popular Sunday periodicals in England would love to hear about. But even on those clandestine trips they had always travelled with a car full of heavily armed security men in front and behind the so-called target vehicle.

He gripped the wheel tighter at the thought of their vulnerability and was glad that he had not left his heavy service revolver behind as he had been ordered. Its hardness in his shoulder-holster was comforting: at least he would be able to give a good account of himself if they hit trouble along this dangerously deserted road. He couldn't allow himself to even think of the possibility of the Provos knowing of the trip and mining the road in the expectation that the car would avoid the main road. It was all bloody madness.

O'Casey glanced at the passengers and again the clear blue eyes were studying him. It was unsettling. He shifted the rearview mirror to avoid the eyes, and gave himself a clearer view of the second man. O'Casey had been briefed on who was to accompany Blue Eyes on this tour, but this man was completely new to him. That was another worrying matter which Dublin had seen fit to pass over. And the accent! Sort of American, but not quite; perhaps Italian, but again not quite. Almost like one of those Chicago gangsters who had been transplanted from southern Italy and raised in America. A harsh, broken accent which juggled the two societies and came out sounding gruff and ominous.

O'Casey had checked him out, as he held open the door for the passengers, when they had started off on their journey, just before dawn. Using the gloom as an excuse he had jostled the American-accented man, skilfully frisking him as he did so, and was almost disappointed that he wasn't carrying anything under the heavy topcoat. Had he been carrying a weapon, O'Casey would have challenged him immediately and, with any luck, been able to abort this damn, stupidly dangerous, journey.

The American pointed through the front window at something and O'Casey caught a glimpse of a soft, well manicured hand before turning his attention back to the road. Another enigma, he thought ruefully. The soft hands of a cleric on a gangster's body.

Suddenly, an inadequately placed signpost was reached and gone and the blue-eyed man leaned forward to speak. 'I feel the next turning on your left is the one we want to take.' O'Casey nodded silently, annoyed at himself for having missed the sign. As he turned the car onto the gravel path he realised that Blue Eyes couldn't have known the route, he'd apparently never been here before. 'Damn eyes see everything,' he muttered to himself with more than a little admiration for the stocky, white-haired statesman.

The Austin Princess drew to a stop before the large doors of the Abbey. O'Casey stepped from the driver's seat, casting his eyes slowly around the grounds and then across the façade of the building itself. There was no one to be seen; no figures lurking in the bushes; no faces peering through the Abbey's Norman windows. The grounds were empty. Not a sound; the Abbey was completely silent. He unbuttoned his jacket, alerted by the unnatural stillness of the place, and moved to close the rear door.

'It's much too quiet, I don't like it at all, sir.'

The blue-eyed man pushed the door open and stepped out onto the gravelled driveway, stretching luxuriantly. 'Do not fear, my son,' the words came softly, reassuringly from the big man, 'all is as it should be. Wait here, we shall not be very long. Fifteen minutes, no more.'

O'Casey obediently returned to his seat and reached for the radio telephone under the dashboard. He spoke rapidly to the security forces waiting a bare half-mile away. 'Tango One, Blue Eyes delivered. Over.' A crackle of static ran along the airways and he repeated his short message as he watched the man, code-named 'Blue Eyes', walk towards the ancient carved doors and, after twisting the heavy wrought-iron handle, disappear with the American into the cavernous Abbey. The speaker crackled again.

'Understood. How long?'

O'Casey fished for a Rothmans from his silver cigarette case before pressing the 'send' button on the side of the hand microphone. 'Fifteen minutes, no more, he says.'

'Right. Rendezvous Alpha 18 when able to join the tracks. Out.'

O'Casey fired the match with one hand as he replaced the mike. The message had told him several things. Alpha 18 was the back-up rendezvous point, which meant the Colonel in charge feared that outside agencies had got wind of the trip. Joining the tracks meant they were to be met by a full contingent of security forces when they left the Abbey grounds. The slight tremor in the operator's voice told him most of all. He knew Riley was a solid, unflappable man and the nervousness – was it really there or had he imagined it? – indicated they expected something to happen. He flicked the half-smoked butt away and reached for the revolver under his left arm. Without removing it, he released the safety catch, easing the gun slightly in the holster to ensure it wouldn't stick if he needed to draw. As O'Casey climbed out of the car he again ran his eyes over the redstone building and prayed the men would complete their business quickly so they could rejoin the main security force.

Inside, the objects of the security man's concern were hurrying down a long, quiet corridor, which smelt of centuries of polishing by supplicant priests and monks. Without apparent direction, seemingly by instinct, the blue-eyed man turned first this way and then that through the maze of corridors. At length, he stopped before a cell door and nodded to his companion who stepped forward, pushing open the door.

The cell was bare save for a wooden writing desk set in one corner, and a small army-style cot with a single blanket folded neatly with a tiny pillow at one end. The walls were stacked with row upon row of books and high up, there was a single arched window from which hung a crudely carved wooden cross. A bare bulb burned feebly above the small priest seated at the desk who had spent the night poring over the leather-cased volume that lay open before him.

As the two men entered, the priest raised his head slightly and then, without looking at his visitors, he sighed gently and removed his reading glasses. 'It is time then?' he asked sorrowfully. Cardinal Francis Barretta of the New York Archdiocese moved to his side and rested a carefully manicured hand on the priest's shoulder. 'Yes,

Father, it is time. He has come to start you on your sacred task.'

Now Father Giovanni Falangi looked at Blue Eyes in recognition, slid from the stool and crossed the short distance to kiss the Papal Ring. 'Holiness, how I wish that I could have had the honour of meeting with you under different circumstances.'

Pope John Paul raised the priest from his supplicant position and embraced him. 'My son, my son. I too wish that it could be under different circumstances and it grieves me that I must send you forth. I pray to God Almighty that you are prepared and that you will endure.'

Falangi stepped back slightly and studied his Pope's face. Tears coursed down the rugged, deeply-etched cheeks from the pools of blue set beneath the white hair. There was no doubt this Pole cared deeply for his fellow man. Falangi felt uplifted and the doubts that had lingered about his own ability to carry out his mission were washed away by the tears being shed by this saintly figure.

'Holiness, with His help and your prayers I shall win through.'

The Pope nodded gently and the three men clasped each other and began to pray softly. Then, they changed to the early Latin of the Church of St Peter and incanted from the ancient *Book of the Preparation for the Trial*. As their voices lifted higher and stronger, rain lashed suddenly against the small window above them.

It poured furiously. Lightning flashed rapidly, each bolt following closely after the last, the thunder drowning their words. The glass in the window shattered and the wind howled around the tiny cell, buffeting the three men. Books toppled from the shelves and the light bulb burst as the tempest raged around their heads.

As suddenly as it had begun, the storm abated and then was gone as the final 'Amen' was spoken. White-faced and shaken, the three looked at each other. Finally, John Paul smiled, embracing the priest again. 'It has started, my friend. God go with you.'

Falangi kissed the Papal Ring again, and received in return a blessing. He then kissed the Cardinal's ring and shook both their hands warmly. He was ready.

They closed the huge doors of the Abbey behind them and looked around the grey, leaden landscape which pressed heavily in on them. Barretta shuddered involuntarily at the feeling of evil which seemed to stalk them. 'He sees us, Holiness.'

The Pope chuckled. 'Oh yes. This time he intends to be the victor, but, as has happened so many times in the past, he will find that we are more than a match for his evil and the evil of his followers. Father Falangi is well prepared for his task – in him lie all our hopes and all our prayers.'

Barretta was surprised to see O'Casey sitting behind the steering wheel rather than standing solicitously by the passenger door. He imagined the rain had forced him to seek sanctuary in the car and had distracted him from registering their return.

They stepped into the car and with hardly a backward glance O'Casey shot the car forward as though escaping from all the gunmen in the world. Barretta glanced quickly at the Pope who sat impassively in his corner, staring straight ahead.

When the car had travelled a quarter of a mile along the driveway and was out of sight of both the Abbey and the road where they would rejoin the Pope's main escort, O'Casey suddenly slammed his foot on the brakes and swung the car off the road into a small copse. A foetid smell filled the car, causing Barretta to gag, tears welling in his eyes. The car pulled to a stop and O'Casey's head swivelled full circle on his shoulders, while the rest of his body remained facing the windscreen. Barretta stared in fascinated horror as nasal mucus poured from O'Casey's nose. The mouth opened and a flood of bile and vomit spewed out in a torrent covering the Pope. Then the mouth spoke, deep, resonant, almost hypnotic. 'Your mother was a whore, Vicar of Christ. You are a lover of little boys' assholes. Kiss my ass, Vicar of Christ, and enjoy everlasting love between the tits of your fallen nuns.'

Barretta's hand searched in the pocket of his overcoat for the small bottle the Pope's secretary had given him that morning. Suddenly he felt an invisible iron grasp around his wrist, squeezing it tighter and tighter until he feared it would snap. All the while the Pope sat in the back of the car, lifeless save for his lips rapidly moving in prayer to cast back this devil into the pit to which it belonged.

The Cardinal gasped with pain as the head continued to spew its invective at John Paul. A disjointed arm snaked obscenely over the back of the front seat, the hand appearing at once both a hand and a python's mouth. It slithered forward grabbing the Pope between the legs, and a lascivious grin spread over O'Casey's face. 'You like that, don't you, Vicar of Christ? You like me pulling your cock. Want me to suck you off, you old whore-banger?'

Barretta howled in rage at this intolerable insult and with a supreme lunge freed himself from the demon's grasp and hurled the contents of the bottle over the vileness in the front seat.

O'Casey screamed as the holy water found its target and the sound echoed deafeningly around the car. An eye popped from its socket and hung drunkenly down his left cheek, swivelling at the end of its cord. Fat maggots writhed and fell from his mouth and nose, dropping onto the floor, covering it in an instant in a heaving, writhing carpet of putrescence. The head swivelled clockwise, five full turns, suddenly flopped backwards over the seat to lie still finally, looking up at the Pope, who still maintained his impassive posture. At length he crossed himself and opened the door to step out.

As they leaned against the rear of the car limp with relief, two men rushed up, machine pistols at the ready. Barretta waved to them indicating that they were okay. One of the officers spoke rapidly into his walkie-talkie while studying the condition of the Pope's clothes. The second officer looked inside the car. A second later he looked away, unable to bear the scene that met his eyes.

'Jesus, Mary and Joseph,' he muttered, not caring that the head of the Catholic Church stood near. 'What the Devil has happened here?'

Barretta looked at the man and nodded. 'Exactly that, my friend.'

Within minutes a large car pulled up and a tall, military man stepped forward. He surveyed the scene and called over the two officers who had arrived there first.

'You will forget what you have seen from this moment on and you will never talk of it to anybody. Do you understand?'

The taller of the two looked dumbly at his superior and then back towards the car. 'Yes, sir, but what the hell happened? . . .'

His superior held up a hand. 'I said forget it. Understand?' Without waiting for further questions he turned back to the two men standing patiently at the rear of the car. 'Holiness, Cardinal, are you both all right?'

John Paul nodded. 'Thank you, my son, I think we are unharmed physically, our mental torment will be salved by prayer. Poor Mr O'Casey, I was afraid this would happen – that the evil one would exact . . .' Suddenly the words dried up and the Pope walked to the car and touched the dead man and said a silent prayer.

The security chief turned to Barretta. 'He *knew* this might happen?'

Barretta nodded. 'It was a risk we knew we were taking, Colonel. That is why we asked for a devout Catholic to drive us. We felt that such a man would have a better chance of withstanding possession in the first place, but in the event he could not, his spirit would be of greater aid in rejecting the possessive spirit. The Devil and his minions exacted a terrible price, however, for losing this first battle.'

The Colonel rubbed his jaw. 'Well, I don't know about all that, Cardinal, but I do know I have a dead officer on my hands. How do you suggest I handle this situation?'

Barretta smiled tiredly at the Colonel. 'I'm a spiritual advisor, Colonel. This is really more your department from here on, but perhaps you should call for a coffin and have those two men seal the casket with the body inside. Then perhaps you should burn the vehicle for it surely is an unholy thing now.'

The Colonel rapped out his orders to the two hapless men and then escorted the Pope and Cardinal to the larger limousine. As the car roared away, the Colonel threw the two clerics' soiled topcoats into the Princess to be burned with the car after the body of his agent had been removed. He glanced at O'Casey and was gripped by an icy fear as the disgorged eye moved around the cheek to glare malevolently at him. As he stepped away from the car the mouth opened in a wicked smile revealing rats, which scurried out and sat on the cadaver's shoulder.

The car burst into flames and a sudden explosion ripped

the vehicle apart. As the Papal escort sped along the lonely road the sound of the explosion reached them as a distant peal of thunder. Barretta and His Holiness Pope John Paul exchanged grim glances.

CHAPTER TWO

October 1981, Occupied Iran

Tom Mott eased himself gently over the body of the Iraqi soldier aiming his portable electronic news-gathering camera towards the distant puffs, which denoted the position of the Iranian artillery emplacement. If nothing else he was a professional and the assault on the convoy would make news. Particularly, he thought ruefully, if he were to be killed in this latest flare-up in the uneasy peace which existed between the two countries.

Mott wedged the camera between some small rocks and stabilised the lens with the dead soldier's canteen. He began speaking immediately in measured and urgent tones into a small hand microphone. He knew from many years' experience in news reportage that the end result would make good television. The sense of urgency he conveyed in his voice coupled with the film – shot through a close-up lens – would give the impression he was under fire from a matter of yards when in reality the heavy guns were a good five miles distant; a small but permissible deceit in the harsh world of media scoops.

After he was sure he had sufficient footage of the firing guns, Mott lifted the camera and swung it around to capture the burning trucks of the convoy and the perfectly positioned, filmwise at least, bodies of the troops who had died in the barrage. Having done this, he swung the camera towards his own feet in order that the viewer, safe in his living room, could see the dead soldier whose left arm was draped over Mott's boot as though trying to pull the reporter back into the shell-hole. Mott spoke slowly, seriously into the mike about the soldier and then abruptly snapped the cut-off button and replaced the equipment into its cushioned, metal case, all thought of the dead man gone from his mind.

Settling himself comfortably against the side of the hole he waited for the inevitable cease-fire which, if the Iranians followed previous patterns, would come in about half an hour. After that it would be a simple enough matter to establish how many of the troops in the convoy had survived, film the medical attention given to the wounded and a few general interest shots of a trooper trying to restart a stalled vehicle or of an officer looking grimly into the distance towards the Iranian position. The story would rate in all no more than one and a half minutes on the early network news tomorrow and would probably be cut to one minute for the late edition. After that it would be old news, but once again Tom Mott had been in the right place at the right time – witnessing the flare-up of hostilities between the two countries during a period of calm, when most other news organisations had been reducing their reporting teams.

The reporter fished a cigarillo from his bush jacket pocket and fired the small disposable lighter to the tightly packed end. A cloud of smoke billowed above his head and he thought momentarily that it was a dead give-away as to his position, but the thought was as quickly dispelled. Mott felt as though he could stand upright in the sand and wave at the Iranian gunners and they still couldn't harm him.

At thirty-eight Mott had seen most of the trouble spots in the Middle East. He had recently been awarded a special light-hearted citation by the Washington Press Club – The Jonah Award – for his apparent knack of getting to a position just days, sometimes even hours, before the outbreak of a war, civil disturbance or the overthrow of an existing regime.

This knack, a colleague had once called it a curse, had enabled Mott, at the comparatively young age of twenty-eight, to write his own ticket and to dictate to his network just what he would and would not do. By the time he was thirty-five New York wanted him back in the States as network Vice-President. Mott had refused, preferring instead to make news rather than involve himself in purely administrative functions in an ivory tower.

He was honest enough to admit to himself that half of him loved the excitement of war and danger and the acrid smell of cordite floating through the still desert air, assailing his nostrils and prickling the hairs on the back of his neck. In truth, he liked to record the death and destruction he had witnessed over the past ten years. He enjoyed being a remote and detached observer to the terrible carnage which man inflicted upon man.

Half of him did. But the other half could not be so detached. He found that he hated the looks of terror and anguish he saw as two-hundred-pound shells smashed into mud-walled houses; he was repelled by the sight of blood congealing on mutilated bodies accompanied always by hordes of flies and ruthlessly efficient carrion birds. But most of all, he hated the smell of death; the rotting corpses baking in the desert sun, the wriggling maggots oozing in suppurating wounds of the living – wounds which would fester through lack of attention, and days or weeks or months later would just as surely kill . . .

Tom flipped the remainder of the cigarillo away and watched it abstractedly as it arched into the air before falling rapidly to earth some distance away, kicking up dust motes as it hit the desert road. An Iraqi soldier slipped out of his hiding place and scooped up the butt, darting back to safety just as a shell smacked with a deafening noise some ten yards from where Mott had flipped the butt.

The reporter smiled at the man's lucky escape and ran his hands through his raven-black hair. He thought suddenly of Barbara and he wondered idly what she was doing at that moment – not that it mattered, and he didn't really care. He had married too young, before he joined the network, and the marriage had started to go wrong early; she hoped he would join her father's bank, his own dreams were vastly different.

His rugged good looks and sturdy frame had always ensured that he never wanted for young women eager to share his bed and soothe away his troubles. They had always floated to him, drawn by his square chin, finely chiselled features, those deep cobalt-blue eyes which spoke of knowledge beyond his years, and his black, eminently caressable hair. Barbara's resentment of Mott's decision to be an individualist had caused a deep split in their relationship, but a wider one was caused by the knowledge that she would never be enough of a woman for this handsome man.

They hadn't bothered with a divorce and on his rare visits to New York he would stay at her house, without attempting to play the role of husband or father. Within days of arriving he would start making travel plans and within the week she would invariably be driving him to Kennedy Airport, he returning to the life he had chosen and she resuming her place in New York's society world.

Very occasionally he wondered if it would be worth the effort of getting back together with Barbara again; it happened when he thought of Michael, their son, growing up without a real father. However, the rare occasions when his visits coincided with the child being home from boarding school quickly dispelled such conjecturing. Michael was more her son than his!

He scratched hard at his temple to dislodge the worrisome sand flea intent on burrowing into his skin and checked that the equipment was still secure. Roughly five minutes had passed since the last shell had fallen and, if past experiences were anything to go by, it would soon be time for the Iraqis to make a hasty, but reasonably dignified, retreat back to town.

Mott yawned luxuriantly, flipping open the case and withdrawing the familiar camera for the shots which would complete his report. Then it was back to Baghdad for a shower and a long, cool drink before meeting Adnan Hourani. He swung the camera around to capture the troops emerging from their hiding places and spent several minutes shooting footage he knew would probably end up on the cutting room floor, before setting the camera on its tripod and moving in front of it to give his 'on camera' wrap-up. That done, he repacked the equipment and returned to his jeep which amazingly, seemed completely unscathed by the shelling. Luck was still with him. He started the engine and pointed the jeep in the direction of the now departing convoy, heading back along the road to Khurramshahr and the bridge across the Shatt-Al-Arab waterway into Iraq.

'Well, I should say, Tom, that you had a very fortunate escape,' commented Adnan Hourani as he handed his guest a tall glass of bourbon and iced water.

Mott laughed dismissively as he relaxed in the plush couch in the Arab's library. He liked Hourani and thought the two were kindred spirits. Although they had met only recently – collided with each other would be a better description – Mott felt this articulate and highly educated man had enough confidence in himself not to feel threatened by Tom's own strength of character. This had happened all too often in the past and at one time Mott had worried about it but finally accepted that he would have few male friends. Those few, however, would be precious.

He had been browsing through one of the many shops in the crowded bazaar which specialised in manuscripts and objets d'art from the farthest corners of the Middle East. Mott was not an expert, but he did like to collect old manuscripts. He had spent many years studying Arabic and felt that the manuscripts allowed him some insight into the culture and often helped him to explain seemingly unfathomable attitudes and stances to his western audience. Without thinking he had turned a corner in the tightly packed, untidy shop and walked straight into Adnan Hourani, scattering the man's parcels and knocking him unceremoniously to the floor.

After apologies were made, introductions followed and the Arab had insisted Mott spend an evening with him in order to peruse some of the prime pieces in Hourani's collection. That had been three nights ago and now this was their farewell drink before Mott flew to Rome.

'Not really, Adnan, although it was pretty hairy when the shelling started, but I'm beginning to think that I'm indestructible. I've been doing this work for ten years and in all that time I've never had so much as a scratch. I've lost three cameramen, two soundmen and thousands of dollars' worth of equipment – but never a scratch on me.'

Hourani smiled softly and took a chair opposite his guest. 'Then I should say you are due for a big fall with an attitude like that, my young friend.'

Mott laughed good-naturedly at the rebuke. 'You mean because I'm starting to believe in my own indestructibility?'

'Exactly. If I were you I think I should tend to be even more careful in future than I had in the past.'

The two men laughed together and Adnan Hourani

found himself liking this good-humoured man. Under different circumstances they might have become almost like brothers. The thought was quickly dispelled – that could never be. 'Tell me about your family, Tom.'

The question came so suddenly that Tom was amused. So often people in these parts engaged in endless infuriating preambles, wandering right around a subject rather than requesting information directly. His host, instead, had come straight to the point.

'Not a great deal to say on that score, Adnan. As you know, I'm married with a teenage son. That's about it.'

'Parents?'

'Both dead, I never knew them. I was raised in an orphanage. To my knowledge I have no living relatives.'

'It must have been a lonely existence without any family around you, particularly when you were growing up?'

Tom thought for a moment and then shook his head. 'Not really. I was obviously very young when my parents died, a car crash I believe, and the orphanage always seemed quite the most natural thing in the world to me.'

'And you were not adopted?'

Mott laughed. 'No, one of the nuns once told me that I was so big and strong, potential parents used to think I would wreck their houses within a month.'

'It never bothered you, that you weren't adopted?'

'I never thought about it. It didn't seem to matter to me at all that other kids were "chosen". I was quite content to wait.'

'For what?'

Mott looked puzzled at the question. 'I . . . do you know, I really don't know how to answer that! I suppose I always knew that I would be successful one day. It's hard to answer, Adnan, perhaps I felt that it was my destiny not to be adopted.'

Adnan nodded in understanding. 'Yes, I see. Now if

you will oblige me, I have something to show you and a small favour to ask.'

Intrigued, Mott followed Adnan to a large English oak desk at the far end of the sumptuous study. His host unlocked one of the drawers and carefully extracted a thick leather binder, placing it almost reverently on top of the desk. It was fastened by a broad red ribbon which Adnan gently loosened to reveal several layers of protective tissue paper. These in turn were carefully peeled away, exposing what was evidently an extremely ancient parchment.

Tom was transfixed by what lay before him: the parchment was worn thin with age, too fragile, almost, to touch, and covered in an ancient script he could not identify.

'The pride of my collection, Tom,' explained the Arab softly. 'I believe it to be written on human skin, but as to its contents, neither I nor any of my associates have the least idea.'

Tom had extended his hand tentatively but quickly withdrew it when he heard what the manuscript was made from. Hourani stood back slightly, allowing Mott an uninterrupted view of his treasured possession. He studied Mott as he reached for his pipe and started the process of lighting it. Once lit to his satisfaction he moved closer to Mott and pointed to one particular section of writing.

'This sequence of lettering has been identified as uncial, probably fourth century, and as far as I can tell it is a name. Gilgamesh.'

'Gilgamesh?'

'I'm surprised you haven't heard of him, Tom, all children in the Arab world are threatened with him when they misbehave.'

'Sort of a bogeyman?'

The Arab nodded in agreement. 'Yes, but the legends

surrounding Gilgamesh attribute him with much more than being a child's bugaboo. He is supposed to be blessed, or cursed, depending on your viewpoint, with everlasting life. He walks the earth throughout all eternity, standing ready to repel the evil one into the abyss at the pre-ordained times when the portals are opened up for him.'

Mott allowed a short laugh to escape from his lips. 'You talk as though you believe in him,' he chided.

Another match was waved over the pipe bowl and his friend looked pensive for a moment. 'Perhaps I like to think that there is such an entity watching out for the interests of mankind. But I am not alone, many societies, races and castes know of him by one name or another – the most common is The Eternal One – and attribute to him the power to save the world from the great Cataclysm which the evil one wishes to draw us into.'

Mott accepted the offer of a refill. 'I thought only western religions believed battle was constantly being waged between the forces of good and evil. The Koran doesn't dwell too deeply on the subject does it?'

'No, that is true, but Christianity hasn't cornered the market in the fight against the many devils of the Underworld, you know. We Muslims have made the odd contribution as well. After all, my religion is a lot older than yours!'

Tom laughed at the second rebuke of the evening. 'Okay. I'm sorry. Now what is it you want me to do for you?'

'First, can you identify the writing?'

Tom looked again at the sheet and shook his head. 'I can't say I've ever seen anything like it before, Adnan, although the script does look familiar.'

Hourani nodded. 'I know, somehow everyone who sees this parchment says much the same, but apart from the one portion of uncial lettering I'm afraid we have drawn a blank in identifying it and this is where you can be of help to me.

'There is a priest at the Vatican who is perhaps the foremost authority on ancient languages and writings. As you are going directly to Rome I wondered if you would take the parchment to him for his evaluation.'

It was Mott's turn to hold up a restraining hand. 'I'd be happy to take it with me but I will not be back in Iraq for two or three months. After Rome I plan to return to New York for a while.'

Hourani replaced the tissue paper and gently retied the ribbons before handing the parchment to Mott. 'That does not matter. If the priest can give a date and a translation while you are in Rome then please carry it with you until your return to Iraq. If not, leave it with him and I shall collect it from him in December when I have to go to Rome myself. Either way, I am sure it will remain safe.' Tom accepted the commission and Adnan fished inside his Savile Row suit and handed him a small engraved business card. 'I have written the priest's name on the back of my card. I thank you for this service.'

Two hours later, Mott stripped off his soiled clothes and showered briskly, grateful for the efficiency of the westernised bathroom. As he was drying himself he suddenly felt the room grow increasingly stuffy, the heat becoming almost unbearable. That was odd: desert nights were generally cool.

Gasping for air, he wrapped the towel around his middle and crossed to the wall control unit which handled the air conditioner during the day and the heating system at night. He turned the dial to 'maximum' but nothing happened.

Then all at once the light bulb hanging from the centre of the ceiling began swaying gently. He watched in amazement as it swung with ever-increasing force casting terrifying shadows around the room.

There was the sound of running water. Mott ran to the bathroom – the shower had been off – but now water was cascading from all four taps. Even as he watched, the shower spurted back into action, a brown rust-like substance gushing violently from the nozzle.

He backed away, stunned, and a little afraid for once. The ceiling light was swaying more slowly now, but the bulb glowed a deep crimson, bathing the room eerily in a rich velvet colour. Then it burst. The room was quiet and dark, lit only by the light from the bathroom, and the oppressive heat seemed to strangle him. He staggered forward, throwing open the tall French windows which led onto the balcony. A wind howled into the room, tearing the large bath towel from his waist, hurling it like a frenzied dervish to the ceiling high above him. He stood naked, blinded by the fury of the onslaught as the room disintegrated under the ferocity of the tempest.

He struggled to open his eyes against the biting harshness, aware that this incredible wind was now sucking linen, shirts, shoes and anything that wasn't fixed down out through the balcony windows and into the blackness of the night. And then the wind found the precious manuscript folder and lifted it off the bureau.

Mott struggled forward but was driven back to smash painfully into the wash stand in the corner of the room. Frustrated, he gripped the porcelain basin and pushed forward with all his strength to slam the left hand window back into its bracket. With the force of the gale now channelled through one half of the aperture, it appeared to grow in ferocity and Mott felt his strength ebbing away from him.

The folder darted around the room like a trapped bird and Mott knew that if he didn't catch it quickly it could be damaged irreparably by the hard stone walls or worse, sucked through the window and lost.

Then suddenly he had it safely in his hands. Instantly the wind diminished and then was gone. He surveyed the chaos in his room and righted a chair before slumping gratefully into it clutching Hourani's precious manuscript. The air around him felt heavy and the night seemed more grey than the usual black of the desert sky.

From the bathroom the sound of gurgling water heralded the end of the malfunctioning plumbing and a long, slow sigh escaped from Mott's lips as he sat in the chair wondering at the events of the past few minutes.

At length he accepted that the phenomenon had been caused by a freak simoom racing in from the desert and he set about tidying the room. He poured himself a large glass of brandy and, before climbing into the large bed to lie awake half the night in the now cold room, he carefully secreted the folder under the mattress to ensure that it remained safe.

CHAPTER THREE

Second Week in October, Vatican City

Cardinal Barretta sat on the softest couch in Monsignor Molinari's large office and closed his eyes. Weary after the long flight from New York he knew he had aged considerably over the past two years. He felt it more now, the advancing years reducing his stamina, cutting back the volume of work he had managed so easily in the past.

Perhaps the last two years had been a strain on him, he mused as he gathered his thoughts for the meeting, but Falangi must be going through hell every day. His heart felt heavy at the thought of the old priest and for the thousandth time since the Trial had begun he wished that another way could be found. There couldn't of course, he knew that. Ordained at the beginning of time this was the form which the Trial must take. Save for individual interpretations the format must be strictly adhered to in order to prevent mistakes along the way. One error and the results would be too terrible to contemplate.

Molinari returned the ornate telephone to its cradle and left his desk to join the Cardinal on the couch. The two men had been friends for many years, each having a high respect for the other. The Monsignor knew Barretta to be a man who had worked hard in the Church and had been rewarded for his devotion. As a humble parish priest, Barretta had helped to ensure that American Catholicism had not been eroded further by the moral decline of the country. He was unhappy that little growth had been achieved in that country since the end of the

Second World War but, to the Vatican, his work was a success.

For his part, Barretta, a former dock worker who now wore a cardinal's hat, held a deep esteem for the academic ability of the Pope's Principal Secretary. Molinari epitomised the high academic qualifications which were now needed to ensure advancement through the hierarchy and Barretta often voiced how lucky he felt to have advanced from his Chicago parish without so much as a degree in Humanities now that the Church seemed to require priests to have PhDs before performing burial services!

Molinari would debate the virtues of education long into the night with the Cardinal proving, beyond doubt, that in a fast-paced, modern world the priesthood needed men who could tell the difference between a solenoid and a micro chip. 'The day will come,' he had often said, 'when priests will need to know how to pilot a space ship to carry His message and then our present academic qualifications will appear rudimentary in the extreme.'

Their meeting on this fine Italian October day seemed to the casual observer to be a routine one between an American Cardinal and the Pope's advisor. The beams of hot sunlight streaming through the ornate rococo windows belied the sense of urgency they both felt as they sat wrapped in thought.

'You seem tired, Cardinal, are you well?'

'As well as I need to be and yes, I am very tired. But that's to be expected isn't it?'

The younger man cast his eyes down slightly and inclined his head in agreement. 'His Holiness wishes me to convey to you his sincere love and best wishes.'

'Thank his Holiness for me, perhaps we shall meet again once this terrible ordeal is over.' He accepted the coffee from Molinari with a nod of thanks. 'But tell me, how is Father Falangi? Is he still strong?'

Monsignor Molinari rose to his feet and walked slowly towards the window. From his office he could look out over the city at the bustling traffic in the distance and see just below him the moving spectacle of thousands of pilgrims who came to worship at the very heart of the Church. If they only knew the terror which, at this very moment, threatened to erupt around them; if they could but realise the threat to their souls, indeed to their very sanity, and the extent to which the Catholic Church protected them as they went about their daily business. The threat which waited, striving to escape to strike and claim as its dominion the earth and its peoples.

'He remains strong,' Molinari said at last, turning from the window, 'although it seems the attacks upon him gain in force as each day passes.'

Barretta sighed and replaced the coffee cup on the side table. 'It has to be, I'm afraid. Father Falangi knew better than any of us what would be involved. After all, he has spent many years in preparation for this Trial. I do know I could never have conceived of the horrors which have come to me in many guises since the commencement at Dragha Abbey. It has taken all my faith in God and the Church to survive. Falangi must have experienced a hundred times worse than I.'

The Monsignor felt a sudden chill in the room despite the late summer sunshine and he rubbed himself vigorously to ward off both the real and imagined chills. 'His Holiness has asked me to ensure the preparations are complete for the remainder of the Trial.'

Barretta rubbed his hands across tired eyes, selecting those pieces of information necessary for the Pope to know and those better left out. 'We believe we have identified the portal which Satan will use. The date remains the same as previously thought. It is now just a question of ensuring that our Champion is in front of the portal at the correct moment to prevent the forces of Satan from entering Christ's domain.'

The sun vanished as Barretta spoke and the atmosphere grew heavy. It began to rain – gently, then harder, and soon was beating angrily against the glass. In the square below, tourists and pilgrims alike scurried for shelter from the downpour. Molinari crossed the room and turned on the electric light, glad of the comforting glow which spread from the many table lamps scattered about the office.

'And what of Satan's own earthly protector, the cacodemon? What of that heinous creature?'

'It is being tracked at all times, Monsignor. The poor orphan whose body and mind it occupies will, with God's Grace, soon be released from its unknowing possession. The creature will face our own Champion at the time and place ordained. We have taken steps to ensure the cacodemon is sent to the place in plenty of time for Father Falangi to watch over it. Our Champion has also been located and Father Falangi has been fully advised. I think, I pray, all is ready. Tell his Holiness to pray for us all.'

As the two priests talked in soft tones, Tom Mott walked steadily across the most beautiful square in the world towards the west entrance of the Vatican. He ran quickly up the wide granite steps, past the two Swiss guards into the marbled interior of the Vatican Library building. His footsteps echoed hollowly on the marble floor and he felt strangely disquieted to be in this ornate palace of Christianity.

At the reception desk the young priest looked up at his approach and smiled comfortingly at Mott's tentative enquiry in faulty Italian. 'Perhaps you would prefer to converse in English, sir, how can I help you?'

Mott cleared his throat, 'Your English is a sight better than my Italian, Father. I'd like to see one of your librarians as I believe he may be able to date a manuscript I . . .'

'Do you have an appointment, sir?'

'No, but . . .'

The receptionist smiled benignly. 'Then I am sorry I cannot help you. Our experts can only see members of the public who have an appointment. It is not possible otherwise, they are so busy you see. Perhaps if you were to ask your parish priest to arrange one, an earlier date could be arranged,' he ventured helpfully.

'I'm not a Catholic,' retorted Mott, with some irritation. He hadn't considered the possibility of not being able to see the priest immediately and for a moment was at a loss as to what to do. He had been toying abstractedly with Adnan's business card when suddenly he handed it to the priest. 'Can't you explain to this librarian that I have with me a manuscript which names Gilgamesh? I'm sure he would be interested in seeing it. My name's Mott. Tom Mott of CBS News.'

The priest studied the card for a moment, then reached for a hidden telephone and spoke rapidly to someone in Latin. Mott smiled to himself when he heard the dead language being used, wishing now that he'd taken more notice of Latin in high school. He was curious as to how this young man would explain to a senior librarian that a strange and thoroughly soaked American was insisting on seeing him.

'If you will take a seat sir,' said the priest as he replaced the instrument, 'the senior librarian will see you. A guide has been dispatched from his office to escort you.'

Mott sat on the hard bench indicated. Almost immediately a man in a black cassock stood in front of him and asked him to follow. They walked for what seemed an age along wide corridors, his footsteps ringing on slate and marble floors; then along narrow wooden walkways which smelt musty with age; through majestic, double-doored archways and through tiny ones, oak doors studded with nails, seemingly too small to allow passage of a normal-sized man. At last his guide opened yet another door and ushered him inside with a small bow.

The book-lined library had the smell of antiquity. From where Mott stood he was able to look down into the circular room, empty except for one man seated at a large, well-worn desk. The figure turned at the sound of the door closing and waved pleasantly. 'Hello Mr Mott, you will find a metal staircase to your left. Please come and join me.'

The journalist spotted the opening in the metal gantry. Peering down the hole he saw that the metal staircase wound in a circular path down to the floor below. As he stepped from the bottom rung and onto the threadbare carpet the priest hurried forward to greet him more formally. 'My dear Mr Mott, how do you do? I understand you have something to show me from Mr Hourani?'

Mott shook the offered hand and studied the small clergyman, who had greeted him so warmly. The diminutive figure standing before him was no taller than five foot two with a thick shock of white hair. The clergyman's body appeared frail, as though it would take no more than a gentle hug to snap it in two. He had noticed the man walked with a slight limp and a casual glance to the floor confirmed that the right foot was slightly twisted. The face, despite the broad smile, showed evidence of pain. It was as though the agony of mankind was mirrored in his pale grey eyes while each line on his face had appeared through suffering. His hands also showed the passage of time, a web of blue veins, gnarled by arthritis.

Mott could sense that this old priest cared far more for humanity than his own being.

'I didn't realise you knew each other, Father . . .'

'Falangi. Oh yes, I know of him. He has quite a reputation.'

As they walked back to the desk in the centre of the room, Mott quickly surveyed his surroundings. The priest, instead, watched his visitor.

'I see you are wondering how a man can bury himself in a musty old place like this?' Falangi chuckled and the eyes momentarily twinkled at Mott's embarrassment. He gripped Mott by the arm pointing at the rows upon rows of books with a sweeping arm. 'In these books, parchments, scrolls and tablets, on pieces of tree bark and dried river clay are the secrets of humanity itself, the chronicles of man's life, man's dreams and man's religions. In these tomes you could discover the very roots of man, my friend. Why, given enough time on this earth, I imagine you could find here the original lease to the Garden of Eden made out to a young man called Adam and his wife.'

'Okay, Father, you caught me,' Mott laughed. 'I guess I was thinking along those lines. But I'm curious about something . . .'

Falangi perched on the edge of the desk and inclined his head slightly. 'Well, we can't have that now, can we. What's got your curiosity?'

'Your name doesn't match your accent.'

Falangi laughed lightly. 'It never fails, everybody queries that. Well, I'll tell you. My dear mother married an Italian soldier, but she was Irish and that's where I was brought up, in dear old County Roscommon. Now does that settle your inquisitiveness?'

'It does and thank you,' laughed Mott. He liked this little man and was glad he'd been press-ganged into bringing the parchment. If nothing else, he would leave the Vatican after an enjoyable interlude with a delightful Irish-Italian cleric.

Mott placed the manuscript folder on the desk, releasing the ribbons and unfolding the case with the same care which Hourani had taken. The parchment lay revealed and the priest emitted a long, drawn out 'aah' before gently moving Mott out of the way to look at it more closely.

'Hourani says he had identified one portion of writing as uncial . . .' began Mott before an impatient hand was waved to quieten him. The journalist turned his attention to the library, crammed with old and treasured volumes. It seemed a warm place to him, full of the mysteries of ages past. The priest was probably right, you could imagine that the entire story of mankind lay here. Perhaps even the key to the reason for man's existence lay hidden in this very room.

At length, as the shadows stretched across the room, the priest stood erect and looked hard at the American. 'I'm sorry to have hushed you so rudely, but it helps to have no preconceived notions cluttering your mind when studying such a magnificent document as this.'

Falangi looked back thoughtfully at the desk top before continuing. 'Well, your associate is quite correct, a part of the document is uncial, but a greater part than he thought. Only one phrase is pure uncial . . .'

'The name of Gilgamesh?'

'That's right, Gilgamesh. It was a common trick to mix two or even three forms of writing to confuse unauthorised readers. You must understand that, at the time this manuscript was written, the average man was totally unschooled in anything except basic survival techniques. Reading and writing was solely the domain of spiritual advisors and the nobility. These privileged groups were extremely jealous and wanted to protect their own secrets from rival factions. Consequently, whenever something of great importance needed to be written down, it was done in a way which only another member of the group could decipher. A form of early code if you will.'

The priest picked up the manuscript and, with extreme care, lifted it towards the light. A hint of light showed through the browning parchment. 'I wonder if you know what the material is?' he said as he replaced it among the tissue paper.

'Adnan Hourani said he thought it might be human skin.'

'I should tend to agree with him. It certainly isn't paper. Nor is it bark, leather or manufactured from water reeds, much too porous for that! Now, taking into account the subject matter I should say it most certainly is skin. Probably the skin of a poor unfortunate who was executed because he was thought to be in league with the Devil.'

With a faint trace of awe in his voice Mott said, 'Now how on earth can you put all that together in such a short time? It's incredible!'

Father Falangi motioned Mott towards a chair, and reached for one himself before continuing. 'Experience! That's how I know. You see the fabric itself is transparent, the material used in those far-off days was of a very dense consistency, tree bark, slate and so forth. Therefore a transparent material from that period must be regarded as skin of some sort, animal or man. But when you know how easy it was for a citizen to be flayed alive for even the most minor crime you realise the odds are slightly stacked in favour of it being human skin. No animal would be slaughtered just for the skin, you see, so animal skins for writing would be rarer than human.

'I say it was some unfortunate who was accused of being the Devil's confederate, because the message on the epidermis has a religious significance concerning Old Nick himself. Add to that the fact that the writing is a lovely blend of fourth century uncial and ancient Gaelic, Irish variety, and it's a fair bet it was written by the old Druid priests who had a particular penchant for stripping a man's skin for a whole variety of sins, the most serious of which was to consort with the evil spirits.'

The priest leaned back in his chair, studying Mott with an amused glint in his pale eyes. He enjoyed delivering instant appraisals of the old manuscripts which daily found their way to him and enjoyed the slack, stunned expressions on the faces of the people who brought them. If it was a sin of pride, Falangi could justify it by saying it was the sin of a humble man, proud of the great gift his God had bestowed upon him.

'Well, that's pretty good, Father, but the million dollar question is . . .'

'What does it say?' Falangi leaned across the desk as Tom removed his notebook from a jacket pocket and pulled a pen out in readiness. The priest started to trace the characters on the page and in a deep, resonant voice interpreted the words.

'This is the great miracle of Sin,
That has not happened to the Land
Since the days of old;
Launch the offensive, eternal Gilgamesh, capture the Fugitive,
Let the terrifying offensive rage against Him,
Let the winds carry His wings to the secret Place,
Let not sovereignty return to Donn.'

Mott wrote the final sentence in his notebook and looked up at the priest, his handsome face frankly puzzled. 'What does it mean?' he asked.

'That's your real million dollar question Mr Mott,' Falangi answered, his hands shaking slightly. 'The translation of a document is always relatively easy if you know what clues to look for. Understanding what's been said . . . well now isn't that always the way with the thing.'

Tom felt the man was mocking him with his soft Irish accent and grew suddenly irritable. As if reading this change of mood the priest resumed talking in a concili-atory manner.

'Let's take a look at the clues we have. The two names, Gilgamesh and Donn give us the best insight into what the manuscript is revealing. You obviously know about Gilgamesh . . .'

'Yes, he's called the Eternal One in Arab mythology.'

'That's correct, and also by the same name in some of the Greek writings. Now Donn, what do you know of him?'

The black hair shook softly in the almost dark room. 'Not a thing, I've never heard of him.'

Falangi stood and walked unsteadily over to the filing cabinet to switch on the light. The dark room was instantly illuminated by a series of bulbs set in the library's alcoves. Returning to his seat he continued, 'Donn is from Irish mythology and is believed to have lived, perhaps he still does, who knows, on a little rocky island called Tech Duinn, off the west coast of Ireland.

'The important thing about him is he is supposed to be allied to the Devil although there is strong evidence to support other legends that he is in fact Satan himself, not just a servant.

'Now as far as I can determine, this message is concerned with the Devil escaping from Hell – the secret Place – to bring about the great Cataclysm – the miracle of Sin. Now where it says that it has not happened since the days of old, well, that could be referring to our Lord's encounter with the Devil in the desert. You'll doubtless remember your scripture telling us of Christ's Trial which lasted forty days and nights. Conversely it could be referring to a time we don't know of when the Devil ruled on the earth – Let not sovereignty return – or at least of a time when he tried to enter the world through one of his portals.

'The rest of the piece exhorts Gilgamesh to do his duty and repel the Fugitive – the Devil – from the earth back into Hell where he surely belongs.'

'And all this was written in the fourth century? It's really quite remarkable, isn't it?'

'Fourth century? Oh no, much later.'

'But you said . . .'

'I said it was a fine blend of fourth century uncial and ancient Irish Gaelic. Not that it was *written* in the fourth century. Indeed, the Gaelic used here is even older, a great deal older. No, it is a blend of two ancient languages designed to fox readers of a much later period who were not authorised to become involved in the parchment's message.'

Mott scratched through a section of his notes. 'When would you say it was written?'

The Irishman paused briefly and continued, 'If you want a scientific answer I'm afraid you'd have to wait for a full series of Carbon 14 tests to verify the age of the skin and chemical testing of the inks to pinpoint the likely date, although, in fairness, I should point out that this wouldn't prove it hadn't been written last week.'

'I don't understand.'

Falangi stood and stretched himself to ease the muscle spasm which he now felt in his back. He glanced at his watch and indicated to Tom that they should walk towards the exit. As they walked along the winding corridor which led back to the main entrance Falangi explained.

'Carbon 14 dates accurately the *age* of a given object and by examining the composition of the ink we can say whether or not this *conforms* to the known make-up of inks used at the time. For instance, if we found lead in the ink, but no charcoal, we would know it was a twentieth-century ink. Having said that, even if the ink stands up to chemical analysis and has the necessary properties we cannot be sure that the manuscript isn't a forgery, put together by someone who has a thousand-year-old piece of human skin and knows how to make old inks. Carbon 14 will verify the age of the *material*, not when it was written. Do you understand?'

Mott nodded, 'Is there another answer you can give me?'

Father Falangi nodded a pleasant goodnight to the young priest still on duty at the desk and they stepped out into the cool Roman air. 'Certainly there is, a religious one. The parchment is one thousand years old this year. Now if you will excuse me I have a meeting I must attend. It has been very nice meeting you. Goodbye.'

He stepped rapidly down the wellworn stairs, disconcerting Mott by his sudden departure. After a moment Mott called after him. 'How can you be so positive of the date?'

Without turning the priest called back, 'Revelation, chapter twenty, verse three.' And then the small Irish priest with the Italian name was swallowed up by the bustling Vatican City crowd.

Perplexed, Tom crossed St Peter's Square towards the main gates, head bowed once again against the driving rain. He needed a hot bath and a couple of stiff drinks to settle his feeling of unease before joining the station manager of CBS at the Rome Hilton.

Tom Mott felt more relaxed than he had done for a very long time as he pulled the door to his room closed after a long shower. He was looking forward to seeing his friend, Chuck Noble, CBS's Rome station manager. Chuck and he had started at the network on the same day and although Chuck's forte had been the administrative side of news gathering, they had struck up an immediate friendship which had remained firm throughout the years.

A sudden thought crossed his mind and reopening the door he crossed quickly to the bedside table hoping to find a Gideon's Bible there. Rewarded, he flipped through it to page 245, Revelations, chapter twenty and scanned the verse the old priest had named as evidence that the manuscript was a thousand years old. He read it and re-read it until he was sure he had understood. Then he quickly wrote the section down in the notebook before leaving to meet his old friend.

CHAPTER FOUR

Chuck Noble stretched, his dark arms raised high above his head, and leaned back in the swivel chair, grinning broadly at his friend. 'Good evening last night?' he ventured and Mott winked back at the station manager. Without a doubt, a visit to the Rome station was always to be recommended – particularly if Noble was to be your guide around the night spots.

'How does your wife tolerate you, Chuck? I mean so many people knew you last night, particularly the women, you can hardly ever be home.'

Noble's infectious grin bubbled out again and the big man slapped the top of the desk. 'She knows that a man's got to holler once in a while and she knows the job means I got to make connections all over the place. What she don't know is how popular us nigger boys is to the Eyetalian women.' He waved an airy hand before concluding, 'Besides, my Coralie trusts her man.'

The two men laughed and then suddenly Noble was serious. 'Ah well, I suppose we have to get down to some work. What can I do for you, my man?'

The previous evening Chuck and Tom had agreed that not one word would be discussed about business, to enable them both to relax and enjoy each other's company. It had been nearly two years since they had last met and they had a lot of catching up to do. Now, however, the mood was one of business and Noble slipped easily into his role as a senior official of the Network in charge of the large Rome bureau.

'Not a great deal, Chuck. I need some expenses and a first-class ticket to New York. Perhaps you'd better send a telex to Harman and let him know I'm heading for home for leave. There's nothing much happening that I can get my teeth into at the moment, so I thought I'd grab the chance of getting a change of underwear.'

Noble shook his head. 'You can tell Harman yourself, he's in Rome on one of his little fact-finding tours to the front line. Should be in the office in a little while and, by the way, he knows you're here.'

Mott groaned. Although he had carte blanche to travel wherever necessary to gather good news material, vice-presidents like George Harman resented his independence. To Harman the idea of giving a reporter, any reporter, a free rein was anathema to his concept of a well-run, efficient organisation. There was no doubt that if he could, he would enforce the CBS ruling that foreign correspondents rotate their theatre of operations every three years. Mott had no desire to leave his much loved Middle East and North African patch and, so far, Harman had been unable to enforce the ruling.

However, like most administrators, Harman invariably tried to make things just that little bit tougher for his lone wolf. Once in a while the heavy expense chits would be queried or a lengthy message would reach him concerning waste of film, suggesting he might benefit from a refresher course in film editing or camera technique. These were petty annoyances designed more to remind Mott who the boss was than to force him to toe the line.

Tom knew how to play that game as well. Once in a while he would ensure that he was seen in a restaurant with a senior officer from NBC or ABC. The grapevine would buzz with stories that CBS's number one reporter was planning to switch to a rival network. A senior man would immediately be despatched to ensure that Mott was happy and to discuss his upcoming contract – which often had a year or more to run! No, Mott knew how to play the corporate game, but he hated the waste of time and energy it involved. His job was to gather the news, not to fight internal wars with frustrated Veepee's who never got closer to a combat zone than a Brooklyn traffic jam!

'Shit. If you had told me that last night I'd have been on the midnight to New York.'

The happy chuckle rippled out again. 'We agreed no business talk, now you can just face the man like a big brave honky.'

Mott shook his head. 'So long, Chuck, see you next time I'm in town – I'm leaving!'

As he pushed his chair back the office door opened and a small bookish man entered, nodding cursorily to Noble before turning his attention to Mott. 'Well, Tom, leaving before you've had a chance to say hello?'

Mott sighed and perched himself on the corner of Noble's desk. No hand had been offered by either man to the newcomer, nor did he appear to expect it. 'Hello, George, wife let you leave the States again, has she?'

The insult was ignored as Harman eased himself fastidiously into the chair vacated by Mott seconds earlier. He placed his cow-hide briefcase on the polished floor, snapped open the combination lock and withdrew a thin brown folder. Next he positioned a pair of pince-nez spectacles on the end of his nose and produced a slender gold pen, completing the picture of an efficient, well-heeled administrator. Mott and Noble watched and exchanged derisory grins as Harman cleared his throat in preparation to speak. Mott beat him to the punch:

'What's on your mind, George, or doesn't it concern me?'

'It concerns you very much, Tom. First your expenses for the last three months . . . approved.' He selected a piece of paper and handed it to Mott with just the hint of a grimace on his hawk-like face. Mott accepted the cheque with some surprise and glanced over at Noble. His friend shrugged, equally astonished by the ease of the transaction, Mott having a reputation for notoriously high claims.

'Are you going through the change of life or what, Harman?'

The vice-president looked puzzled. 'I don't understand you, Tom. You filed your expenses and they have been paid. Is the amount wrong or something?'

Mott folded the cheque and slipped it into his pocket. 'The amount is correct, it's the "or something" which bothers me. Normally you have at least a caustic remark to make. This is so unlike you.'

Harman leaned back in the chair and studied the two men expansively. 'Let's just say I have come to the conclusion that it would be beneath you to cook your expenses. I'm sure your claim was fair and just . . .' Noble snorted and turned away. '. . . And therefore there is no reason not to settle outstanding claims quickly.'

The mood in the room relaxed. Harman quickly ran through the various other items he wished to talk to Mott about, explaining he preferred to deal with them while he was on his tour of the stations, rather than having one big session the next time Mott was in New York. He greeted Mott's news that he planned to leave for New York that evening with what appeared to be genuine pleasure. 'I'm sure you deserve a break, Tom, and I'm equally sure that lovely wife and family of yours will welcome having you home for a while. Enjoy yourself.'

And then the folder was returned to its briefcase, the business concluded. Harman replaced his glasses in their tortoiseshell case and suggested they all go to lunch. Although preferring to eat alone with his friend, Noble accepted the invitation quickly, knowing it to be politically expedient. As Harman turned towards the door, Mott glowered at his friend, who grinned an apology.

They walked past the bank of chattering telex machines which sped the latest news from around the world, even the noise conveying a sense of urgency. Suddenly a messenger rushed up to Harman and handed him what was evidently an important message flimsy. Harman scanned it quickly and frowned. 'No reply at the moment, thank you,' he muttered to the operator.

'Trouble?' enquired Noble casually.

Harman shoved the message into his pocket, 'Nothing serious, but it does screw up some long-standing plans. Burrowes has been injured in a car crash.' He held up a hand to forestall Noble's questions. 'He'll live, concussion and a few broken bones, but nothing internal, thank God.'

They got out of the elevator on the ground floor and walked the two blocks to Sammy's Bar and Restaurant on Via Giovanni Lanza, a favourite meeting-place for the world's press. They quickly found a booth and Noble pressed Harman for more details about the accident. As Harman studied the menu he related the additional information.

'He was on assignment in Ireland for a special we planned to run in two weeks' time. It seems the car had a blowout and Burrowes woke up in hospital. The driver was killed.'

Open-faced sandwiches and beer were ordered, and the three chatted casually, Harman filling them in on Rome's society figures about whom he seemed surprisingly knowledgeable. At length, in a break in the conversation, Mott asked a question which had been preying on his mind. 'What's this special about then, George?'

Harman looked up from his sandwich, puzzled. 'Special? Oh, the Irish thing!' he spooned more mayonnaise onto his plate and dipped the sandwich into it before continuing. 'We've been running a series on mythologies from all over the world for the past few months called "This Strange World". It's proved to be very popular with both sponsors and the public. Burrowes was to film a segment for next season.'

He sank his teeth into the sandwich, munching appreciatively as his colleagues waited impatiently for more details. He took a perverse delight in the dramatic pause.

'An old festival, Samhain, takes place on November first – sort of Irish version of Hallowe'en as far as I understand it. We had arranged to film the festivities – you know the sort of thing, modern harmless high jinks connected to old Druid festivals. Weenie roasts instead of sacrificial virgins!'

Noble poured himself another glass of beer from the jug and drank noisily, obviously pleased with himself despite Harman's look of reproach. Mott accepted a refill and waited. He knew that Noble would relate the story in the same way that he normally conducted fiscal negotiations.

'So what's this festival all about? I mean Guy Fawkes night in England celebrates the uncovering of a plot to burn the Houses of Parliament, is this the same sort of thing?'

'Oh, no, Tom, quite different. It seems the Irish believe Samhain is the date, the only date, when the Devil can enter the world from Hell. According to tradition, the rites they perform will keep him back, but as they don't know which year he will try to escape from his inferno, they keep this day sacred by practising their mumbo-jumbo every year just in case. Of course, it's turned into a party these days as most people have forgotten the real reason for the festivities.

'Our researchers discovered that a village called Craghan is the only place in the Republic where they actually conduct the ceremony in the old way, at one of Donn's alleged portals – a place called the Cave of Cruachu.'

'What? What did you say?' demanded Mott.

'The Cave of Cruachu.'

'No, before that. The name . . .'

'Donn?'

'That's it. You know two days ago I'd never heard the name and now this is the second time. Tell me more about this place, George.'

'Well, I'm not an expert on the story, Tom, but as I understand it this cave place has got quite a reputation with the locals. Strange happenings have been reported around the mouth of the cave as far back as people remember; fierce beasts, demons and so forth. People are alleged to disappear if they venture on the hillside after dark. I suppose it's much like the Loch Ness Monster thing or our own Big Foot legends.

'According to the ancient Gaelic priests the Cave of Cruachu was the place where Satan, or Donn as he is known in Ireland, would re-emerge after being imprisoned for the statutory one thousand years. That's about all I know, I'm afraid.'

A cold chill ran through Mott and he muttered inaudibly to himself. Harman leaned forward, 'Did you say something, Tom?'

'I said Revelations, chapter twenty, verse three: "And cast him into the bottomless pit and shut him up and set a seal upon him that he shall deceive the nations no more till the thousand years should be fulfilled and after that he must be loosed a little season." '

Noble whistled in admiration. 'Hey man, I didn't know you could spout the Good Book.'

'I can't. An old priest pointed me to that passage in reference to something else, but it's an incredible coincidence, that's for sure.'

The three lapsed into silence. At length Harman cleared his throat and looked slyly across the table at his talented reporter. 'Er . . . I don't suppose you'd care to take over from Burrowes, would you, Tom? It would only mean postponing your leave for a few weeks, four at the most!'

Noble and Mott exchanged glances and then collapsed in paroxysms of laughter. Helpless, they slumped against each other as their merriment rang out through the noisy restaurant, causing other diners to turn to see who it was enjoying themselves in such an unrestrained manner. Mott dabbed at the tears of laughter, while Noble tried unsuccessfully to contain himself by drinking a glass of beer. He spluttered and choked as another giggle rushed up his throat, and sprayed beer over Harman.

The hapless vice-president's expression of injured innocence set them off again and it was a full three minutes before they were sufficiently in control of themselves for Mott to risk replying.

'You're a crafty bastard, Harman! All that bullshit in the office . . . paying the expenses so quickly, Jesus, I thought you must have a motive, it was so out of character.'

Noble sighed as the final threat of giggles died. 'I bet the message he got had nothing to do with the Irish story. That's class! Man, that's the sort of thing we wouldn't have given him credit for.'

Harman sat patiently throughout the exchange between

the two men. In a strange way he was pleased that they praised the deception. Any appreciation of his talents, no matter what form it took, was to be welcomed.

'Be that as it may, Tom, will you do it? We really are in a hole on this one. If we have to scrub this segment we'll lose something like thirty thousand dollars doing a replacement film, and on film already shot.'

Mott shook his head. 'No! I'm already planning my vacation period. Besides, you know I don't like to do documentaries like this. Hard news is my bag, not light entertainment for fat-arsed Middle America!'

The sallow-skinned waiter cleared the table of debris and brought a second jug of beer. Noble refilled their glasses, waiting for the next round of Harman's argument. It would probably, he thought, follow the line of letting the Network down at a time when it most needed Mott's assistance.

'Damn it, Mott,' snarled the executive, all trace of pleasantness gone, 'we don't ask much of you while you're chasing around doing your own thing. Just once in a while we would like a little gratitude from you, to show you remember who you goddamn well work for. I could order you to do this show, you know!'

Noble glanced at Mott and raised an eyebrow slightly at the familiar tightening of the left cheek muscle in his friend's face. That was not the best approach to take with *this* man!

The words came softly, penetrating the clamorous din going on around them. Delivered in a carefully measured tone which conveyed an anger that left Harman white-faced.

'Perhaps, but you won't. I'm the most experienced war correspondent you've got. I doubt you'd do anything to make me go over to ABC or NBC. Second, don't ever threaten me again or challenge my loyalty. You tried the sneaky way to get my interest and it didn't work. Leave it at that!'

An uncomfortable silence reigned around their booth and Noble rapidly thought of a way to break the stillness. 'What about Michaelson in Paris, or Johannsen in Moscow? Couldn't you pull them for a month, George?'

'Both on assignments too important to curtail,' came the short reply.

'Well, then, somebody from New York. You must have someone available in Current Affairs or Light Entertainment.'

Again the short answer, forced from between tightly drawn, angry lips. Then: 'The new schedule is keeping *everybody* busy. Without new programming, even the prima donnas will be looking for work!'

Abruptly the man pushed himself clear of the booth and with a perfunctory 'I'll see you in the office, Noble,' he stalked from the café. Noble blew out a long breath at the acrimonious departure and eyed his companion.

'You know something, man?'

'What's that?'

'He's mad as hell!'

'How'd you know?'

'He didn't pick up the bill after inviting us to lunch!'

The two laughed and any discomfiture between them evaporated. 'Hell, Chuck, I'm not cut out for that type of crap. It might have been different if he'd come right out and asked me.'

Noble stood in the gangway peeling off lira notes from his billfold and looked askance at his friend. Mott shrugged. 'So it wouldn't have been different, what the hell.'

They stepped out into the chill air and stood for a moment enjoying the freshness after the smoky restaurant. Noble fished inside his shirt pocket and extracted two cigarillos, handing one to his colleague. 'What now, Tom?'

Firing his lighter, he waved the flame first under Chuck's and then his own cigar. 'Back to the hotel to pack and get ready for the airport. You going to drive me?'

Noble nodded and indicated they should cross the busy Via Merulana towards the Piazza di Santa Maria Maggiore. The negro drew his topcoat tight around his throat and cursed the unseasonal weather. 'It doesn't normally start raining until late November. I think you've brought bad luck to my city, old buddy.'

Mott grunted agreement and looked around at the heavy grey sky. He'd thought how the weather had deteriorated since he'd left Iraq and, for a moment, he wished he were back in the heat of the desert rather than squelching through cold Roman puddles. On entering the piazza Mott noted with pleasure the sight of a church standing before them, solid and reassuring. 'What's that one, Chuck?'

Noble, huddled against the rain, glanced up briefly. 'Another church as far as I'm concerned,' he muttered unhappily as a new raindrop found its way inside his collar. 'If you're at all religious you could have a real ball investigating Rome's churches; there's 450 of the goddamn things. Place is full of religion!'

Mott had grown into the habit of taking constitutionals after lunch and was amused at his friend's evident discomfort. 'Seriously, which one is that?'

Chuck Noble had the reputation of knowing all the major tourist sights and many of the more obscure ones with an intimacy rivalling that of the official tour guides. He made it his business to become acquainted with whichever city he was posted to better than the average citizen. Mott had been with him in London once when

Chuck had argued long and hard with a taxi driver over the best route from their hotel to Heathrow Airport. Noble had won both the argument and the grudging respect of the driver, who moaned that it had taken him years to build up his knowledge of the city.

'It's the church of St Mary Major or, in Italian if you prefer, Santa Maria Maggiore. Legend has it that one night in August 352 the Blessed Virgin appeared before Pope Liberius and ordered him to build a church on the spot where he would find a heavy unseasonal snowfall the next day. The church has five doors, the one we are approaching is called the Holy Door. Inside are several priceless works of art. Do you want to take a look so that I can get out of this damn rain?'

The plea went unanswered as they reached the entrance and Tom stopped to look around the piazza and up at the church. It was magnificent. 'No thanks, but I appreciated the potted biog.'

Noble sniffed. 'You're welcome. If you're really into churches you should see San Clemente. Now that really is something . . . LOOK OUT!'

Chuck had glanced upwards, towards the high roof of the church, studying three large statues carved in the shape of angels. The centre one appeared to be looking down at them, wings spread, and this had captured his attention when suddenly he yelled his warning, pushing Tom hard in the back and propelling him forward onto the wet pavement. As Tom hit the ground with a bone-jarring thump he rolled instinctively to both lessen the shock of slamming into the granite square and to remove himself further from whatever danger Noble had seen. He came to rest on his back some ten feet from his friend.

Noble was still staring skyward, a horrified look on his face, immobilised by the action of pushing Tom away. As though in slow motion Tom looked up at the church to witness an angel with wings outstretched swoop down towards the spot where moments ago he had stood next to his friend.

His mouth opened to scream a warning, but even as the first syllable was uttered it was too late. Half a ton of masonry smashed onto Noble's upturned face and Mott felt the splashes of warm, sticky blood hit him, even as Chuck crumpled to the floor under the weight.

The next moments were bedlam as the slow motion snapped into a thunderous present; screams from a group of Japanese tourists mingled with the immediate siren of an ambulance racing to the scene, summoned by an unseen witness; hands at first pulled him to his feet and then restrained him from moving towards the broken body protruding from under the statue.

Mott stood motionless, his eyes transfixed by the dead body and the figure of the angel, which had crushed the life from it. A broken wing had forced through Noble's skull and exited through his back causing the body to list awkwardly, unable to lie flat in death. Blood oozed from the smashed corpse to flow down the four marble church steps. Fragments of bone mixed with brain matter were splattered obscenely against the centuries-old Holy Door, sliding snail-like down its length.

Tom looked around the throng as though expecting one of them to offer an explanation. Why should the statue choose that particular moment to fall from its place? Why, after all these centuries should the cement finally release its hold to send the angel hurtling to the square below?

The police officers pressed the morbidly curious crowd back and a solicitous officer took him by the arm. 'Signore, are you hurt?'

Mott looked at the man. He hadn't thought about it, he never needed to think about it. Once again death had been so very close and he had emerged unscathed. For a fleeting moment he thought that he should be sorrowing. Shouldn't he feel something for his friend? But he didn't. His best friend was lying before him, crushed and lifeless, because he had saved Mott's life and he couldn't feel anything – no remorse, no sorrow, not even gratitude. He just accepted it.

'I'm fine, thank you,' he muttered after a moment. He turned away, looking past the crowd over the piazza towards the hurrying afternoon traffic. Funeral arrangements would have to be made. Inquest to attend. There would be no flying to New York that afternoon. The police paperwork could take days to clear up.

As he turned back to the police officer he caught sight of a familiar face in the crowd but for the moment he couldn't place it. Perhaps he had seen him in a shop or possibly the hotel. Suddenly he had it – the priest from the library, Falangi!

Staring at the man he noticed that he was wearing an ordinary suit and tie and had donned a transparent grey mac to keep out the drizzle. Why did it bother him? The Vatican was reasonably near. He turned for a final look at Noble's body before it was covered with a sheet to await the coroner. Suddenly it occurred to him. A man had been killed and the priest should have come forward to administer the last rites. It was his sacred duty!

Mott whirled around and searched the sea of faces for Falangi, but he had gone, swallowed up by the restless crowd. Even as he scanned the people moving away, searching for the grey mac, a black-coated priest pushed his way through the crowd and hurried over to the corpse.

In the distance a peal of thunder announced there would be no break in the bad weather which had arrived so early this year. Mott turned his attention to the policeman who waited, patiently, for the expected report.

As they talked, the coroner arrived and made a superficial examination, giving permission for the body to be transferred to the city morgue. As the ambulance raced noisily away Mott thought of how right Noble had been. He had brought bad luck to the Eternal City.

The following five days passed like a blur to Mott. As he kicked the door closed in his room at the Cavalieri Hilton, he breathed a sigh of relief that the funeral was over and that the Italian bureaucracy had found itself capable of dispensing with the business of the inquest relatively quickly.

He had reported back to the bureau office as soon as he had been able to do so and Harman efficiently stage-managed the myriad of details to be handled following Noble's sudden death. Mott had volunteered to take on the unenviable task of telling Coralie Noble. Harman had agreed, but had also assigned a female colleague to go with him on the premise that a woman would be invaluable at a time like this. He had been right.

Coralie, uncontrollable in her grief, had asked over and over why it should have been her husband and not Mott who was killed. He hadn't been able to answer that and, unemotional as ever, had left the two women together. He caught a taxi back into the heart of the city and stopped the cab when he spotted a likely looking café, which was near enough to the hotel to be convenient, but far enough to avoid being spotted by any messenger sent from the police or the office. Although he still felt no particular grief over the death of his friend, he did feel the need to be alone.

At the sidewalk café he watched the pedestrians hurrying about their business and the endless stream of traffic, oblivious of the angry glances the waiter gave him each time he was summoned from the warmth of the café to serve the crazy American who preferred to sit in the rain.

Eventually he returned to the Hilton to find yet another police officer waiting impatiently for yet another statement. And then the inquest and more statements and, at last, the body was released for the funeral. Coralie weeping, asking Mott to forgive her for the things she had said and Harman coolly efficient, organising the proceedings and making things happen with the least amount of fuss. If nothing else, Mott was grateful to his boss for being so competent in this crisis.

Moving from the door he tossed his jacket onto the armchair before pouring himself a half-glass of scotch from an unopened bottle of J&B. Glass in hand he crossed to the window and looked out over the seven acres of parkland surrounding the hotel, towards the bright lights of the city. Almost directly in front of him stood the illuminated shape of St Peter's. The sight reminded him of the strange little priest.

Turning, he moved about the room collecting his things into a neat pile ready for packing. There was no longer any need to remain in the city and he planned to catch the next morning's Pan Am flight to New York after calling to say his last farewell to Coralie.

Socks were neatly folded one into the other and laid on top of crisp underwear which, in turn, was placed on top of neatly pressed, folded shirts still in their protective cellophane wrapper, emblazoned with the Hilton motif. Once he had completed this task he took a steaming hot shower, soaping his muscular body with his own non-perfumed soap and then rinsed off with jets of ice-cold water.

His body tingling, he lathered his face and quickly shaved. He splashed a little Aramis onto his strong face and, refreshed, examined himself clinically, deciding he still maintained the body of a man much younger than his thirty-eight years. No slackness around the face, no loose skin around his waist or under his arms to sound warning bells. He was fit, perhaps fitter than he had any right to be. He was not a vain man and took no particular pleasure in the sight of his body. It was simply a machine which enabled him to function. A better machine than most, perhaps, but a machine nonetheless.

He dressed in a pair of grey worsted slacks and tailored pale blue shirt, completed with a St Laurent silk tie. He selected a jacket which complemented the outfit and ensured that he had sufficient money. He didn't particularly feel like eating, but he was well aware that if he missed his evening meal he would feel ravenous by the time the flight left in the morning.

Before leaving the room to take the elevator to the roof-top La Pergola restaurant, he lifted the mattress to check on the Hourani manuscript. It was still there, and for a brief moment he considered taking it to the concierge and having it put in the safe, but changed his mind. There was no need, he decided, and within fifteen minutes he sat relaxed and comfortable in the intimate restaurant, closing his mind to the events of the past five days.

The sound of the telephone woke him and in an instant he was alert to the new day, refreshed as always after a bare three hours' sleep. He answered the persistent ring, cordially thanking the operator for the early morning call. He stepped from the bed and stretched, easing the stiffness from his bones, all trace of tension gone. He looked back at the bed and decided he would let her sleep.

The girl had been pleasant enough. Swedish tourist

who had had a little too much to drink, but who had been available and had signalled this fact to him. After a pleasant dinner and several dances he had suggested they go to bed and she had agreed with equanimity, as if he had suggested a casual stroll in the night air.

Mott showered and dressed casually for his flight. He checked the bathroom and bedside table drawers systematically for forgotten items before crouching at the side of the bed to ferret under the mattress for the folder. He probed with his arm, annoyed that the weight of the girl prevented him from lifting the mattress up.

He pushed deeper: nothing. He knew that the manuscript couldn't have moved that far between the box springs and mattress even with the pounding they had given it during their love-making. Enraged, he yanked savagely at one side of the mattress lifting it into the air and depositing the unfortunate girl naked on the floor. She sat up and screamed at him.

Oblivious to her protestations, he scanned the box springs and then dropped to his knees to look under the bed itself. There was nothing. Not so much as a ball of fluff met his anxious eyes. It was gone. He turned back to his suitcase and examined his travel folder. It was complete, even down to the valuable passport. He next checked his precious camera equipment and was relieved to find it all in place in the protective, unlocked metal case. He leaned back thoughtfully against the dressing table.

The girl now stood in front of him demanding an explanation. He collected her things and shoved her into the bathroom with a curt order to dress and leave.

As the bedroom door slammed shut behind her he was on the telephone telling the desk he had changed his plans and would require the room for a further few days. Then he called room service and ordered a light breakfast.

While he waited for the breakfast trolley he thought about the theft, trying to evaluate how it could have come about. The fact that his expensive camera and passport had been untouched indicated that it was no ordinary thief at work the previous evening. There was no doubt in his mind that the thief was after one thing and one thing only – the Hourani document – and incredibly that put suspicion squarely on the priest who had examined it. He was the only person in Rome who knew of its existence!

Across the city, as the weak fingers of early morning sunlight gently touched and explored the quiet street, another early riser peered through a window in a small villa overlooking the racecourse, off the Via delle Campannelle. The roar of an aircraft passing overhead en route to Ciampino Airport was a comforting sound and the little priest said a silent prayer of thankfulness that the long, torment-filled night had at last passed.

Father Giovanni Falangi turned from the window, moving downstairs to the neat, familiar kitchen to prepare his meagre breakfast. As he plugged the coffee percolator into the wall socket he noticed his hands were still trembling and made a concerted effort to stop the shaking which he knew would soon become uncontrollable.

Out of habit, he selected two bread rolls from the basket left by an unseen nun before dawn and poured a steaming cup of thick, black coffee before sitting down at the table.

He nibbled half-heartedly at one roll, but replaced it on the plate with the other untouched piece of bread. He had no appetite. He hadn't since . . . how long was it? Two years now! A long time to be without his former enjoyment of good food which had endeared him to a succession of cooks.

Falangi sipped the coffee gratefully and rooted through an overcrowded pocket for his crumpled pack of English cigarettes. The acrid smoke burned a harsh path into his lungs forcing him to cough painfully at the sudden assault. It was really too early to smoke, he normally didn't bother until after his evening meal, but after the horrors of the past night he felt the need for the tobacco. Perhaps the pain racking his protesting lungs served to reassure him that he was still alive.

At length he stubbed out the half-smoked tube in the ashtray and poured himself another coffee before returning upstairs to the prospect of a hot bath.

Falangi leaned painfully over the Victorian-style white enamelled bath, turning the ornate taps to allow the boiling water to gush out of the fish's mouth which served as the water spout. He still felt the kicks he had suffered from the demons during the night, demons sent by Satan to deter him from his holy task. As the steam filled the large room he limped to the waist-high sink to prepare his shaving things.

His reflection glanced back curiously at him from the wall mirror and he, in turn, stared at it indifferently. He had been shocked in the beginning to see the change. The fiery red hair, showing his Irish heritage, changing in a matter of days into its present snow white; the handsome middle-aged face which had favoured his mother and yet hinted at the Italian in his veins, now ravaged by the horrors he had endured; the clear eyes which had twinkled so readily with the merriment of life – now, for the most part, tear-filled. He picked up the cut-throat razor he'd been given as a young man and which he still preferred over electric or safety razors. He was glad to see that his hands were now quite still. His hands! Perhaps his greatest regret was the deterioration of the fine slender hands which had glided over the ivory keys delighting audiences with his favourite piano concertos and bringing transitory pleasure to the down-and-outs in the Bowery slums. The hands which had been so at one with the piano through God's given talent, now found even the most rudimentary of functions almost impossible . . . With effort, he lathered his face to begin the painful process of shaving, listening to the familiar sound of the bath tub filling.

Suddenly the smell of decay and rot assailed his nostrils and he groaned resignedly as the words reached him, spoken in a deep voice and with a malevolence that caused a sharp chill to race up his spine.

'Feeling sorry for yourself, whoremaster? Why not end it all – slit your throat with the razor and put yourself at peace.'

The priest turned slowly, not knowing what to expect this time. Each visitation was different. In the beginning it had been subtle forms sent to disturb him. Gradually the wispy shapes in the night air had taken a more tangible form and childhood terrors of spiders had been reborn as malformed creatures crept and crawled their way onto his bed. Lately the demons of Satan had been more horrible and spiteful, testimony to the Devil's growing impatience as the Day approached.

The demon sat, neither in the bath, nor on the edge. It appeared to perch on top of a floating morass of excrement which now poured in a never ending torrent from the fish's mouth. Falangi gagged: the stench was unbearable. The demon itself was a misshapen wretch, with scabrous sores covering it from head to toe. Clearly visible on its back were two enormous humps and a thick horn extended from its forehead, curling upwards slightly. A lascivious, expectant grin played on lips which were drawn back to reveal rotted stumps of teeth. Even at this distance,

Falangi could feel the foetid breath emanating from the monster as it breathed in long, rasping gasps. The creature's skin was yellow-green and its arms waved to and fro across the surface of the sewer it perched on, as though waiting for an opportunity to scoop up the excrement and hurl it at the revolted priest.

And then, from between its legs, a massive organ slowly raised in a repulsive erection. As broad as a man's arm, the throbbing, blue-veined member stretched upward until the tip of the penis touched the creature's mouth. One arm snaked across and, as it spoke again, started masturbating in a measured, almost hypnotic manner.

'End it all, priest. Draw the blade across your throat and painlessly find peace and salvation with the true Master.'

Falangi cried out loud at the exhortation to commit a mortal sin and condemn his soul to everlasting torment. 'Foul thing of the accursed Satan, servant of the fallen, begone from me in the name of My Lord Jesus Christ, the true Saviour and son of God Almighty. Begone from me in His name!'

The demon laughed with a broken crackling which reverberated around the tiled room as it pointed its free hand at Falangi. The priest's right arm moved upwards against his will, the razor glinting as it caught the light, and an unseen force steered the dreadful weapon towards his white neck. 'Let's see your fucking god prevent this, asshole sucker!' Unstoppable, his hand was compelled to his own throat, the finely honed blade-edge pressing into his Adam's apple. The force held it there while the entity exhorted Falangi to draw the blade across the throat himself.

He felt the strength draining from him as he stood there in the macabre tableau. He was so tired of it all and so longed for a rest from the evil beings which tormented his body and soul. Perhaps it wouldn't be so bad to end it. Who could blame the man for not having the strength to withstand more pressures in two years than a thousand others would face in a thousand lifetimes?

The demon now sat and sucked his own penis, waiting expectantly, the slanted, evil eyes mocking, encouraging.

Falangi had a fleeting moment of clarity when he was revolted by the thought of suicide and in that moment he prayed desperately for guidance. All at once he was given the strength to step backwards and reach, with his left hand, for the small tumbler of water he kept permanently at the ready in each room in the villa.

As his fingers clutched at the plastic beaker the demon's eyes flashed red, fear showing on the distorted features. It withdrew its member from its mouth and masturbated frantically before aiming it at the priest at the very moment Falangi, with a supreme effort, hurled the holy water. It splashed over the demon, who screamed with hatred and pain and ejaculated, flooding the priest with a cascade of hot, sticky semen. Then the demon dissolved in a haze of sulphuric smoke and fresh water again pumped from the fish's mouth to mix with the sodden excrement in the tub.

Falangi lurched to the toilet bowl and vomited, emptying the contents of his stomach in tortured heaves. He reached for a towel to wipe away the semen from his face and stumbled to the bath to turn off the taps, averting his eyes from the brown effluent which threatened to flood over the brim.

Shaking, he stripped off his soiled clothes and stuffed them into a plastic garbage bag for burning. He stepped falteringly into the shower and turned its sharp needles of water onto his defiled body. After a full ten minutes he dressed in clean clothes and walked to the lounge where he fell to his knees and prayed to his God for forgiveness at his momentary weakness and in thanks for his deliverance.

Overhead, another jet aircraft screeched its way towards the airport, its passengers, blissfully unaware of the events below them, watching the final scenes from *The Exorcist*.

CHAPTER FIVE

The taxi driver swung onto the Via Leone IV gunning the little Fiat at breakneck speed along the wide boulevard, running with the contours of the Vatican City walls. The handsome young Latin ignored two buses converging menacingly towards the centre of the road, forcing them to part only slightly with a blast from his twin klaxons. The taxi shot through the opening without so much as the slightest attempt at braking. For the third time since leaving his hotel Mott came close to regretting having informed the young man that he was in a hurry. On given the instruction to hurry, the Roman taxi driver had changed from a reckless drone into a maniac, intent on earning the larger tip which those in a rush invariably paid.

Mott looked through the window of the car as it continued its journey and wondered how he would approach the priest over the theft of the Hourani manuscript. He didn't really imagine that Falangi would know anything. After all, he mused to himself, as the cab swung into the Via Di Porta Angelica, a priest was hardly the sort of man who could, or would, break into a hotel room. A door key had been used to effect entry which indicated a professional thief. But it was unavoidable. The priest must have imparted his knowledge of the parchment to someone and it was *that* someone Mott wanted to meet.

The cab slammed to a jarring halt. The young man turned with a broad smile, 'St Peter's. Not bad eh?' He spoke in English learned from Hollywood movies and English tourists. Mott grunted noncommittally while he peeled a generous handful of notes from his billfold, thrusting them into the upturned hand with a curt 'ciao'.

He stood momentarily on the edge of Bernini's colonnade gazing at this masterpiece of Italian Renaissance art. The enormous square was surely the most beautiful in the world, an immense space which could hold as many as 400,000 people, surrounded by a magnificent quadruple colonnade, topped with a balustrade upon which were mounted some one hundred and forty statues of saints. Tom proceeded across the square, passed the two breathtaking fountains and stopped briefly to gaze up towards the top of the 85-foot obelisk brought from Egypt by Emperor Caligula in AD 38.

He felt the rain start again and stoically buttoned up his coat to the neck and quickened his pace as he rounded the Swiss Guards' barracks at the eastern arm of St Peter's and along St Anne's Gate, which took him past the Vatican Press building and the main post office. Even at this early hour, tourists wandered along the narrow walkway, oblivious to the weather, cameras clicking and managing to get in the way of hurrying Vatican workers.

To his left, as he crossed the Via St Pio X and headed for the Apostolic Library, rose the Apostolic Palace and as he glanced towards it a peal of thunder crashed directly overhead and a torrential downpour cascaded from the black, swirling heavens. Cursing softly, Mott ran the last hundred yards to the library building avoiding the already forming puddles as best he could.

Once inside the building, he removed his raincoat and towelled his face with a tissue before walking towards the information desk. An elderly clergyman sat at the station calmly trying to explain to a group of German tourists why part of the library building was closed to the public while repair work was being carried out. Mott waited impatiently while a fat *hausfrau* tested her elementary Italian on the hapless man, who in turn struggled kindly to help.

It was apparent that the debate over the section the Germans wished to visit was going to take longer than Mott was prepared to wait. He cast a glance towards the two Swiss guards at the door and, after ensuring they were not watching, casually turned away from the desk and walked purposefully but without hurrying, down the long corridor towards the oval library. Although he was probably breaking all manner of rules, he reasoned that Falangi would be shocked enough at his news to understand the indiscretion.

Unerringly, Mott retraced the route to the library and after three minutes in the labyrinth of corridors, he found himself once again in front of the small oak door studded with square, black nails. He grasped the heavy iron handle and, after a slight pause, pushed the door open, stepping through onto the metal gantry which ran around the top of the room.

His first thought was that his normally acute memory had finally let him down and that he should retrace his steps to discover where he had taken a wrong turn. But almost at once he sensed he had made no such mistake. There was no error.

The shelves which stood groaning under the weight of ancient books were gone; there were no bookcases standing so closely together that a man had to walk sideways between them; no mustiness from books which had lain undisturbed for years; no desk in the large room and definitely no hunched form of the librarian. The place appeared even larger than he remembered it as he stood on the parapet gazing down in bewilderment at the cavernous depths of the empty room.

His mind raced as he retraced his steps to the front hall and approached the now solitary priest. 'Excuse me, do you speak English?'

The receptionist looked up and smiled. 'Certainly sir, how can I help?'

'I've just been to the oval library to see Father Falangi and the room is empty. Can you tell me where he's moved to?'

The priest's face held a puzzled expression. 'Oval room? I'm sorry sir, but there has not been a library in that room for a great many years, several centuries in fact. It has a great damp prob . . .'

Mott interrupted him exclaiming loudly, 'That's rubbish. I was in there last week with Falangi and it most certainly was a library then!'

At the sound of the raised voice, one of the Swiss guards stepped forward, but was waved away by the priest. 'Calm yourself sir, please! I assure you that the room has not been used for a great number of years. Neither have I ever heard of a Father Falangi. I am sorry! Now unless there is anything else I suggest . . .'

'Yes there is, could you check with your administration office on the present whereabouts of this Father Falangi? It's of extreme importance that I locate him!'

The priest turned to the telephone while Mott relaxed slightly. He didn't understand exactly what was going on in this place and felt the sooner he traced the whereabouts of Falangi the better. After a few moments' conversation the priest turned back to Mott. 'The only record we have of a Father Falangi is one who was with our New York Diocese until 1958 and with the Brothers at Dragha Abbey in Ireland until two years ago. Strangely, we seem to have no record of his present whereabouts, so it is likely he has taken leave of absence – for personal reasons, perhaps.'

The American received the news with disbelief. Had he been the victim of an elaborate hoax designed to relieve him of the Hourani manuscript? If so, the thieves had gone to a great deal of trouble in setting up the library when any third-rate burglar could have easily pirated the manuscript, as indeed had been proved, from his room. But what of the priest – Falangi – had he been a fake as well? Mott remembered the scene outside the church where Noble had been killed. He had been surprised that Falangi hadn't come forward to administer the last rites to the dying man. Perhaps he had been an impostor after all.

But even that didn't make any sense. Hourani had written the priest's name on his own business card. It appeared the Arab had been set up long before Mott had come on the scene. Mott shook his head; that didn't work either because the crooks couldn't possibly have known he was on his way to Rome with the parchment. Unless of course, Hourani himself had tipped them off. But why would Hourani want to steal his own property? Nothing made sense!

'The Father Falangi you mention, do you know what age he would be?'

The priest consulted his scratch pad. 'Why yes, he was born in 1933.'

Mott looked disappointed. The age difference was too great. His Father Falangi was a great deal older than fifty . . . or was he? He thanked the young man and apologised for his heated behaviour before turning away from the desk, his head churning with confused thoughts.

He walked, without purpose, from the environs of the Vatican, his analytical mind seeking to thread its way through the mass of inconsistencies. He passed the market place with its yelling, bawdy stall holders vaunting their goods, not noticing them. He turned and walked through narrow streets and dark overcrowded alleyways, overhung with tiny balconies fighting each other for space, then blindly passed little doorways dating back to ancient Rome which housed sharp-eyed shopkeepers and artisans carrying on centuries-old family businesses.

After two hours of aimless wandering Mott found himself in a small square, surrounded on three sides by the ubiquitous outdoor cafés which despite the drizzle still managed to attract customers under their bright, multicoloured canopies. Along the fourth side of the square were several shops catering to the affluent tourist trade which flooded this city throughout the year. He spotted a bookshop and, on impulse, entered the brightly lit shop and asked if they had a road map of Ireland. The pretty assistant flashed her eyes at the handsome American and delayed finding anything of value until she realised disappointedly that he wasn't going to proposition her. Handing him a Time-Life book of Great Britain and Ireland, she accepted his American Express card, still displaying her more prominent attributes in lingering hopefulness.

Mott took the book and settled himself at a table just inside the door of the café opposite and quickly checked the index for Dragha Abbey. It listed a Dragha on map page 259, reference Lh. He turned the pages and in moments had pinpointed the last place Father Falangi was known to have been by the Catholic authorities.

The journalist stared pensively through the window, watching raindrops fall from the edge of the restaurant's canopy. A sullen waiter had brought him a carafe of wine and he sat sipping from his glass for several minutes, oblivious of the lunch-time crowd now rapidly filling the small restaurant, before making up his mind about his next course of action.

He paid the bill and tucked the book of maps under his

arm before again stepping out into the unseasonal weather which had hung over this city like a forbidding mantle ever since he had arrived. The raincoat was again rebuttoned to the collar as he cast his eyes around for a taxi to take him to the CBS office. He would tell Harman he had changed his mind about doing the Irish story.

Settling himself in the back seat of the hurtling taxi he re-opened the book to the map he had marked and traced a line from Dragha Abbey, south east, a mere twenty-odd miles, to the small village. He felt again the slight chill which had run along his spine at the familiar name of Craghan.

As the Dublin bound aircraft lifted off from Ciampino and swung north over the Catacombs, Tom Mott stretched his legs in the first-class cabin and waited for the 'No Smoking' panel to blink off before lighting a cheroot. After a further pause the seat-belt warning light also went out and he gratefully unclipped the restraining webbing.

Far below him, Rome stretched out in a glorious vista as the first traces of autumn sunshine caressed the Eternal City. It was ironic, he thought, that as soon as he leaves the sun decides to shine!

The Aer Lingus stewardess handed him the first-class menu. Without looking at it, he ordered a steak and a bottle of indifferent red wine. As the plane reached cruising altitude Tom remembered Harman's amazement at his change of mind which now sent him speeding to another assignment rather than chasing the sun to New York.

'I thought you said you didn't do documentaries like this. Too facile or something,' said the man, as Mott came straight to the point after returning to the office.

'Never mind that, George, do you still need someone to do the job, or not?' he had demanded, irritated by the sarcasm. When the vice-president had admitted he'd been unable to cover the feature, Mott had asked about the staff he could expect on the filming.

'Two technicians on loan from Radio Telefis Eiren – soundman and cameraman. The camera operator has doubled as researcher. You can leave your ENG here and pick it up on your way back from New York.' The following day Mott had said a curt goodbye to Harman, who had dropped him at the airport, and strode through the bustling concourse for his flight.

As the aircraft increased thrust to carry it across the Mediterranean, into the French traffic corridor, an ornate telephone jangled quietly in the Vatican. Monsignor Molinari reached for the receiver and listened intently as the soft voice told him Tom Mott was airborne.

He thanked the caller, then depressed the cradle for a moment, released it and dialled a number which connected with the small villa on the other side of Rome. It rang several times before a tired voice answered with a single 'yes?'

'Father Falangi? I have news for you. Satan's cacodemon will be at Craghan by tomorrow afternoon. Our friends at the Columbia Broadcasting System have made the necessary arrangements to ensure its positioning at the correct time.'

Molinari waited for a long moment for a reply. When it didn't come he felt a momentary spasm of fear. 'Father? Are you there?'

The tired voice came slowly. 'Yes, Monsignor, I am here. I understand and thank you. I shall make my own arrangements to leave Rome.' Almost as an afterthought and in a tone which seemed to plead for release from this duty, Falangi added, 'Pray for me Monsignor. Pray for us all.'

The connection broken, Molinari gently replaced the telephone and sat at his desk wrapped in thought. And as the afternoon shadows crept into the room the still figure of the man could be seen, hands clasped in fearful prayer.

CHAPTER SIX

Wednesday, 21st October, Republic of Ireland

The immigration officer compared the person in front of him with the likeness in the green passport and then looked casually, with apparent friendliness at Mott.

'And would you tell me what your purpose is for visiting Eire, sir,' he asked with the lilting accent peculiar to all Irishmen.

'Business. I'm here to do a documentary for CBS News.'

The officer stood upright. 'CBS News is it? Well now, is that American or not?'

'That's right. My home office is in New York.'

The immigration officer nodded in agreement and leaned forward conspiratorially. 'Well now, sir, if that's the case would you be telling me how it is that you yourself have just got off the flight from Rome which is in Italy and a powerful long way from your United States. Would you tell me that now?'

An amused smile crossed Mott's face at the officer's confusion. 'I could tell you that I flew the clipper service to Rome in order to catch the afternoon Dublin flight, because there wasn't an alternative flight direct which could get me here sooner.'

Again the nod of agreement from the officer. 'Ah yes now, well you could say that, but it'd be a lie now wouldn't it?'

'I was in Rome seeing an old friend and this job came up, so here I am. If you want to know the ins and outs of my entire itinerary, I arrived in Rome from Iraq. Before that . . .'

'Iraq is it? Well isn't that one of those funny regimes that is always going around blowing things up and supplying the wherewithal to others to do the same in peaceful countries?'

Mott became exasperated. 'Look mac . . .'

'It's *officer* to you mister.'

'Officer. I'm sorry. Look I'm here to do a documentary for my network. Before that I was in Iraq to cover a news story. Before that I was in Liberia – so what? I get around. I'm supposed to get around, for God's sake, it's my job! I can hardly be tarred with the same brush just because I visit a country the Irish Government doesn't think too highly of, now can I?'

This explanation seemed to work as the officer reopened the passport and stamped it perfunctorily, handing it across the desk to Mott. 'Well, all right now, but you mind how you go while you're in our country. We've enough of the lads making trouble without any foreigners comin' in to do the same. Away with you.'

As Tom stalked away from the desk towards the automatic luggage carousel and customs, the officer left the desk and walked to a wall-mounted telephone and dialled three numbers. After a moment it was answered. 'Your feller's just goin' through, sir.' He then replaced the receiver, returning to his desk singularly incurious as to why the Security Service had ordered a special watch for the arrival of this American.

Customs posed no additional problems for Mott and he walked gratefully through into the main concourse of the airport which bustled with impatient figures dashing for taxis. Harman had told him he would telex ahead to make sure he was met by one of the free-lancing members of the Irish broadcasting service, but as far as he could see there wasn't a sign of anybody who fitted the role of newsgatherer turned official greeter.

He dropped his case on the ground outside the terminal building and waited. Sooner or later, he reasoned, either the cameraman or the soundman would appear in a breathless state, apologising for the traffic. Either that or he would tire of waiting, hire a car and make his own way to Craghan to give the crew a lesson in punctuality!

The area around the terminal rapidly emptied in the early evening quiet period as fellow travellers were collected or escaped in waiting taxis and soon Mott found himself almost alone on the sidewalk outside the building. Not a patient man at the best of times, he thought he had been forgotten by two Irishmen who were probably even now closeted in a pub somewhere, and the thought infuriated him.

Decisively, he picked up his suitcase, turning towards the car rental desk inside the building, when suddenly a squeal of tortured tyres reached his ears and he turned. Entering the wide approach road to the airport was a small red sports car being driven with great skill. Mott watched the rapid approach of the vehicle and knew instinctively that this was the car he had been waiting for.

'I'm so very sorry I'm late. I got involved and completely forgot the time,' came the blurted apology as the car slithered to a halt beside him. The driver leapt out to open the trunk for Mott to deposit his suitcase.

Mott remained rooted to the spot, an amused smile playing about his lips. 'I wish I was the passenger you're late picking up, lady, but I think you've got the wrong guy.'

The girl looked quickly around her. 'Aren't you Tom Mott from CBS?'

He nodded, 'Yes, but . . .'

She indicated towards the trunk. 'Throw it in then, I'm

afraid I'm it . . . late and all. I gather they didn't tell you in Rome that you'd got a *female* cameraman.'

Mott cursed Harman under his breath and placed the suitcase in the MGB. He certainly hadn't been told about the girl and there was a very good reason for Harman omitting that detail from his briefing.

Four years previously, CBS had lost a court action in Washington over their policy of not hiring female technical staff for foreign theatres. Within six months Lauren Ashley had been assigned to him while he covered the Angolan war. They had been captured by a gang of rebels led by three British mercenaries and Lauren had been subjected to the most brutal of gang rapes at the hands of the guerrillas before she had taken her own life by slitting her wrists with a piece of sharp bamboo. After he had himself managed to escape, minutes before a government artillery barrage had obliterated the camp, he had sworn never again to work with a woman. Harman had known that.

'I'm Alana Kennedy, 36 years of age and, even if I say so myself, a bloody good cinematographer, so take that sour look off your face!'

He studied the girl while he took the offered hand. She was quite breathtaking! Deep, rich auburn-red hair tumbled in waves down her back to a slender waist; her delicate, high-cheekboned face radiated warmth and exuberance while her mouth parted easily in a ready smile revealing gleaming white teeth. Mott stared at her transfixed while her hazel eyes danced and twinkled as they returned his appreciative scrutiny. His eyes travelled from the smoothness of her neck down to her cleavage where ample breasts jutted invitingly from her half-buttoned blouse and he felt an immediate flush of uncontrollable appreciation, bordering on lust, for this perfectly proportioned woman.

'If you've finished surveying the merchandise, perhaps we'd better get on,' she said in her light, musical voice. Mott nodded his head in a movement that indicated neither embarrassment nor contrition – it was more a gesture of postponement.

He opened the driver's door for her and she slid into the seat with a grace and fluidity which drew his eyes to the skin-tight, faded blue jeans she wore.

'Where to?' he asked, his voice resuming its customary crispness.

'I thought you'd like to rest up in Dublin before we head out into the boondocks. I've booked rooms at a nice little hotel on O'Connell Street. Perhaps this evening I can show you the sights of Dublin.'

Her scent assailed his nostrils and he felt the blood rushing to his head as his mind took him past the intimate dinner and the short sightseeing tour. He was sure she would be no stranger to a man's bed and the thought excited him. It had been a long time since a woman had turned him on in this way and sitting so close to such a sensuous woman for a long journey would be almost unbearable.

He sighed in resignation. 'Forget it, head straight for Craghan, we've got a lot of work to do. I assume you have accommodation booked for us somewhere there?'

She too sighed and gunned the engine. 'Yes, we've rented a holiday cottage just outside the village. Doyle, he's your soundman, is already there.'

The little sports car sped away from the airport and within minutes Alana had located the fast northern route around the city past Dunsoghly Castle to pick up the road to Mullingar, which for part of the journey meandered alongside the Royal Canal. From there they would cut north to Longford and on reaching Tulsk, just over the

Roscommon county line, would drive due north the short distance to Craghan.

The journey passed uneventfully, with all attempts at conversation abandoned after it became apparent that, with the top down, the wind snatched away any but the most shouted of questions or answers. Mott settled down to view with impartial interest the glory of the Irish countryside which was, by now, bathed in the rapidly setting sun.

Shortly before nine o'clock, Alana sped through a small village with a cheery 'nearly there' and pulled over beside a picture book cottage which wouldn't have looked out of place on an Irish Tourist Board poster. 'Home sweet home,' she announced as she bounced still fresh from the car with a liveliness which made the cramped form of her passenger wince.

A man who Mott took to be Doyle stepped through the doorway of the tiny building and lounged against the porch with one hand thrust deep into his pocket, the other clasped around a large tumbler. He studied Mott with deep, coal-black eyes and a face which appeared to Tom incapable of showing any emotion. Instinctively Tom decided he didn't like him.

Doyle stepped out of his way as he moved into the cottage and looked around. The interior was larger than he'd expected. Most of the ground floor was taken up by the lounge which was comfortably furnished, a welcoming fire burning in the large open fireplace. Beside the hearth was a small door leading to the kitchen and to the far right of the room an open-tread staircase leading upstairs.

Mott ducked his head under the old black beams of the living room and moved to the fire to warm himself. As the front door closed he turned to face his two colleagues. 'Seems adequate,' he said glancing around the room once again. 'You're Doyle?'

The slimly-built man nodded agreement and after a pause moved across the room and perfunctorily shook Mott's hand. Alana laughed lightly. 'There now, Doyle. That wasn't so bad was it?'

Doyle grunted, flopping into a chair beside the fire and looking up at the journalist. 'So what does the hot-shot reporter have for us then?' Mott noted the barely concealed antagonism in his face and knew he would have to assert himself right away if he was to ensure he completed the assignment on time. He would also need their fullest cooperation if he was to be able to slip away to investigate Dragha Abbey. From his years of experience, Mott knew that cooperation could be achieved either through fear or through a willingness to succeed.

He turned slowly and glared ominously at the smaller man. 'I don't like your tone, mister! Now we either do this thing my way or you can get the hell back to Dublin right now and forget about working for an American network again. Any more stupid talk like that and I'll boot you off the assignment anyway. You understand!'

Doyle shrugged noncommittally and Mott leaned down and hauled the hapless man to his feet. 'I said, "Understand?" ' The words rang flat and menacing.

'Okay, okay. Jesus Christ, there's no need to act like a friggin' gorilla!'

Mott smiled without warmth. 'Good, we understand one another. I'm the boss and we'll get along fine if you both do what's expected of you. Now then . . .' he flopped into the chair vacated by Doyle, 'what about shot lists, Alana?'

For the next hour Alana filled him in on the scenes she felt the network wanted for the show, explaining competently why she had selected one angle of the story over another and how her notes, which would accompany the film, would allow New York to edit the film correctly and fit in the voice-overs which would add an extra dimension. As she talked, Mott could see that her shot list had been designed by a professional who, on realising they were running short of production time, had rejigged her schedule to allow for a perfect blend of studio work and outside film work. The result would be a well balanced, entertaining programme.

At length, he was satisfied and after making a few minor suggestions to improve the clarity of the story he agreed that both script and shot list were acceptable. He then turned to Doyle, all thoughts of their previous unpleasantness forgotten.

'Do you have everything you need?'

'More than enough tape. I've already done some recordings on a "B" reel which the network can edit into the film as they need to – things like milk cans being loaded into carts, market day chatter, cattle auctions, that sort of thing. Irish background and accents which your sound library probably hasn't got in stock.'

Mott was impressed. 'That's really good. It's those little things which make all the difference to a film like this.' He looked at his watch and rose from the warmth of the chair. 'We'll start first thing in the morning with the sequence of the dawn coming up, illuminating the entrance to the cave. Might as well get the early shooting over with first in case we run into bad weather later on.'

Alana stood. 'Wouldn't you like me to fix some supper for you? You must be hungry after your flight!'

Mott shook his head and with a nod to Doyle, he walked up the stairs to his bedroom. Alana had already unpacked his bag and as he slipped naked between the cold sheets he wished that she was with him now.

He clicked out the bedside lamp and the last thought he had before dropping into his customary deep sleep was of Doyle flashing Alana an angry, envious glance as she offered to fix some supper. He was going to be trouble . . .

The following morning Mott rose an hour before dawn and, after waking his two assistants, set about the kitchen preparing a light breakfast of scrambled eggs for the three of them. Doyle staggered into the kitchen fifteen minutes later, bleary eyes testifying to his lack of sleep. He informed the American that Alana would be down directly and, as the words were uttered, she bounced into the warm room with a cheery smile.

'For Christ's sake woman,' grumbled Doyle through sleepy eyes, 'it's the middle of the night – I feel like death itself.'

Mott chuckled at the man's discomfort and lifted the bubbling pot of fresh ground coffee from the hot stove, placing it together with the cooked eggs on the table. 'Come on, Doyle,' he said brightly. 'I thought you hot-shot soundmen were always raring to get at it.' He winked at Alana and forked a mouthful of creamy egg into his mouth.

Doyle made a wan grin and reached for the strong, aromatic coffee. 'Touché you bastard,' he replied half seriously, but partly in acceptance of being the butt of their humour.

Alana polished off her breakfast and poured a third cup of coffee for herself before looking appreciatively at Mott. 'That was good, thanks. I must say I'm impressed with your ability to get up so easily after a long day *and* cook a delicious breakfast.'

Mott shrugged. 'You have to in this game, or you tend to miss the interesting shots. As far as cooking is concerned, I learned to take care of myself a long time ago. Everybody ready?'

Within minutes Doyle's somewhat battered, dark blue station wagon was backed out of the garage and the three set off towards the Cave of Cruachu and their first sequence of shooting which would head the film. The script had been loosely put together in such a way that as the sun rose over the nearby hills, gently illuminating the entrance to the cave, a voice-over would intone a suitable, attention-getting phrase about this cave having been here since the dawn of time. It was an old and rather stale trick, but it did tend to grab the attention of the viewer and, hopefully, prevent him from switching channels.

Although the senior of the trio, Mott elected to sit in the back seat, directly behind Doyle, rather than in the passenger seat. He reasoned that from this position he would get a better all-round view of the countryside through which they were travelling.

They reached the Craghan crossroads and swung left towards the hills. As they did so, a shadowy figure stepped from the side of the road waving a red torch at the vehicle. Alana peered through the gloom. 'It's the Garda,' she said, as the vehicle rolled to a stop.

'What's that?' enquired Mott as he sat upright.

'Police. Hello Patrick, what are you doing out so early?'

The torch holder stepped towards the passenger side and a black peaked cap intruded into the car. The face wore a serious expression which visibly relaxed when he recognised the girl. 'Miss Alana, well, what in the blazes are *you* doing about so early?'

Alana laughed, jerking her thumb over her left shoulder at Tom. 'This is the boss; we're going up to the Cave to do some early morning shooting for the film. What's up, Patrick?'

The police officer ignored her question and flashed the torch momentarily on Mott and then tipped the corner of his hat with a finger in salute. Tom had seen enough to recognise that something serious had happened. Further along the road he could see several squad cars and an unmarked, white panel truck. Without doubt that would be the coroner's vehicle. Several of this fellow's colleagues were searching the grass verges on either side of the road, while others were stringing white tape around the trees to mark off an incident-spot.

'You've got a death on your hands, officer?' he enquired at last.

The torch flashed back on his face quickly. 'Now then, what makes you say that, sir?' came the soft suspicious voice.

Tom waved the torch away. 'Coroner's van, but I've seen enough police operations to know this is more than a road accident. What's going on?'

'A murder. Young Betsy Connolly. Her parents reported her missing when she didn't come home from her job at the pub. We found her just after three this morning, and I'll tell you I've never seen anything like it before in all my born days.'

Alana cast a glance at Doyle and the soundman nodded imperceptibly before stepping out of the car and walking to the rear to unlock the hatchback. Alana opened her door and flashed a smile of thanks to the policeman who courteously helped her out.

Mott remained in the car. This wasn't his story, although he understood that Doyle and Alana would want to shoot some footage for their own network. The police officer protested when he realised, too late, what the pair were up to and Tom called him back over to the car.

'They're newsmen, officer. I doubt you can stop them from filming.'

Grumbling, the constable leaned against the car and surreptitiously lit a cigarette, cupping it in his hands so a senior officer wouldn't spot the infraction. 'Ah, I suppose not, but even if I could I wouldn't know how to say no to a girl as lovely as she! Have you known her long, sir?'

A pale light crept over the distant hill and Mott silently urged the two to be quick. If they didn't start filming within ten minutes they would lose the dawn. 'No, since yesterday. I'm filling in for the chap who got injured.'

The Garda officer nodded. 'Ah, now would that have been Mister Burrowes? Silly accident that was indeed. The driver must have fallen asleep at the wheel, so he must. Bloody silly place to pick, worst bend on the road!'

Mott stared through the window at the growing light, impatience welling inside him. 'If they get too close they'll be sorry, so they will,' said the officer after a moment's silence.

'What?'

The officer slid into Alana's seat. 'The body was in a terrible, awful state. She'd been raped all right, but the bastard had really worked her over. Blood everywhere. And the look on her face is something I hope never to see again.'

'Local guy do it?'

The officer looked through the windscreen at the returning crew. 'I shouldn't like to think so, not from a friendly little village like this one. More likely to be a passing motorist who saw her walking alone late at night, or someone who's just visiting the village!' His words hit Mott with the impact with which they had been intended and he groaned inaudibly. The last thing he needed was to become involved in a murder enquiry, suspected because he was a stranger.

Doyle returned the equipment to the cases and slammed the rear door before silently sliding back behind the wheel. He looked white and shaken. Alana took her place, waving a farewell to the officer as Doyle slipped the vehicle into gear and drove carefully past the stationary police cars. They had gone a quarter of a mile when Mott broke the silence. 'Not pretty, eh?'

The driver flashed a look in the rearview mirror, suspicion in his voice. 'Now how did you know?'

'The officer told me. Was it really bad?'

Alana shifted in her seat, turning to face him. 'It was horrible. That poor girl, who could have done a thing like that? I could hardly hold the damn camera I was so . . . God, her poor parents!' She turned back and stared through the windscreen in silence. Mott wondered whether she would be capable of doing her job. It was unfortunate about the girl, but to Mott the most important thing was to complete this assignment, not give way to pity for an anonymous young girl, brutally murdered.

They caught the dawn. Just. Alana was totally the professional again as she set her camera for the half-light and prepared the auxiliary lights which would be necessary once they had filmed the weak sunlight touching the mouth of the cave and when Tom would go 'on-camera' for the initial introduction to the site. By eight o'clock they had wrapped it up and returned to the cottage. Doyle expertly released the film cassette from Alana's camera while she made a pot of coffee, announcing he would rush the film back to the newsroom in Dublin. As they drank their coffee, Alana made hasty notes for the editor to string together a report for the twelve o'clock news and then added a note promising to telephone before eleven o'clock that morning with any additional information she could glean from the local constable and doctor. When Doyle left the cottage, he paused momentarily and flashed a glance first at Alana and then towards Mott. The look was not missed by the journalist and he caught its significance. The soundman was warning Mott that no harm should come to the woman.

As the sound of Doyle's station wagon receded, Alana

walked over to him and looped her arm through his as though it were the most natural thing in the world to do. 'Right then, unless you have any real objections do you think we could just clear up the loose ends on this story before we get back to yours?'

He felt an urge to sweep her off her feet and carry her up the stairs to bed. With Doyle gone it was a perfect opportunity to see whether she would respond. He snaked an arm around her waist and drew her supple body towards him, crushing her mouth against his with an intensity which surprised him. The embrace was returned hungrily as her tongue eagerly sought his. She pressed hard against him, gently rubbing her groin against his own excited body.

She pulled away from him, breathing deeply. 'Ooh yes. I can think of nothing better to do right now.' She turned and walked towards the stairs without looking to see if he followed and moved with an urgent grace up the stairs to her bedroom.

Undressing rapidly she stood at the foot of the bed as he shed his own clothes. When he had kicked away the last of them she slid down his body and took his erect member deep into her wet mouth. He gasped with the pleasure, moving slowly back and forth on his heels to heighten the sensation, waves of deep, powerful pleasure washing over his body as first her tongue and then her teeth ran over the tip and along the shaft of his throbbing penis.

When he thought he could stand it no longer, he reached down for her and in one movement lifted and carried her to the double bed and sank his own head in her wetness. She clawed at him and he swivelled his body around so that his legs extended past her head. Their tongues probed and caressed each other's cavities in a frenzy until, at last, she begged him to enter her.

He drove deep into her, thrusting with a force which drove her wild with excitement, and her cries of pleasure became louder as their wet bodies came together again and again.

Tom caught sight of their reflection in the mirror and the tableau excited him even more. Alana's beautiful hair flowed out over the pillow in waves of glory and her whole body seemed to float in the ecstasy of their lovemaking. Suddenly her body arched and her moans stopped for a single moment before he felt the flooding warmth bathe his stiff member deep inside her and at the same moment he too released and their fluids mingled together as they collapsed in each other's arms, utterly spent.

As Mott lay there he realised that in all his life and after all the women he had known, he had never experienced such passion or such wonderfully exhausting pleasure.

The sun crept higher in the autumn morning and they slept.

Doyle left the RTE offices and walked purposefully across the street to Barnay's Bar, a seedy run-down establishment owned by a former news editor who had finally seen the light, deciding to surround himself with his favourite beverages rather than work for the network. The bar was keenly populated by thirsty newsmen, more because it was convenient than because of its cleanliness or decor.

Doyle pushed open the grimy door and allowed his eyes to adjust to the murky interior of the small bar. He spotted the man he was there to meet. Threading his way towards the table at the back of the bar he thought to himself how little this man had changed. But then, it had only been two years.

'Good morning, Colonel, how are you?' he asked coldly

as he dragged the hard-backed chair from the table to sit down. Colonel Ambrose raised his head from the newspaper he had been reading and beamed at his operative.

'Doyle! How very good to see you. Do sit down, I'll order you a drink. Still whiskey, I assume?' Without waiting for confirmation he called to the barman and ordered drinks to be brought to the table.

'Well now, and how are you these days?'

Doyle thanked the waiter and sipped the golden liquid before looking back at the speaker. 'Cut the crap, Colonel!'

The newspaper was brusquely folded, a businesslike manner replacing the friendliness of a moment before. 'Very well, as you will. I take it Mott has arrived?'

'He's arrived,' confirmed Doyle, raising his eyebrows slightly. 'And he's a nasty piece of work if you ask me. Very sure of himself.'

A laconic smile spread over the Colonel's features. 'But most Americans are, my dear boy. Now, what do you know of the little unpleasantness in the village this morning?'

Doyle gave a brief report on what he had seen, adding that the network now had film on the aftermath of the incident. 'If I hadn't seen it, Colonel, I would never have believed a body could look like that – that a person could have been subjected to such terrible treatment. But how does that all tie in with this Mott character?'

The Colonel thought for a moment before answering. 'I'm damned if I know, Doyle, but it seems very strange to me that on the very evening he arrives in the village, a pretty young girl is savagely raped and murdered. Particularly as there has never been a similar incident in that district before. It tells us something, doesn't it?'

Doyle's brow furrowed. 'What?'

The Colonel looked at the man in surprise. 'Why, that

it could well happen again. Oh, yes, I think it may be highly dangerous to be around the man and I do counsel you to be extremely careful.'

The two lapsed into silence. The Colonel waved again to the waiter to bring additional supplies. 'You retired at what time last night, Doyle?'

'About twelve. After Mott and Alana had turned in.'

'And you heard nothing?'

'Not a thing until Mott woke me just before dawn.'

'Up and about that early, was he?'

Doyle made a face at the thought of their early start. 'Bloody right he was! Cheery as anything. Looked as fresh as a daisy. Didn't look like he'd only just got up – too wide-eyed if you know what I mean.'

The officer looked pensively again at Doyle and slowly nodded. 'I do indeed, Doyle. I do indeed know what you mean.'

As they left the bar Doyle turned. 'The thing I can't get out of my mind was the look of pure horror on that girl's face. It was a frightful sight.'

Kid gloves were carefully pulled over strong hands and fingers, the trilby set at the correct angle before the taller of the two men replied: 'Take the greatest of care, Doyle. I appreciate what you're doing for us, but I would hate to think I have put you in any unnecessary danger. If you get in deep water, I want you to get right out. Do you understand?'

Doyle laughed. 'I think I can handle myself, Colonel. Don't you worry about that!'

Abruptly, the soundman turned on his heels and hurried away leaving the Colonel standing at the street corner staring, with concern, after him. Finally he turned away, muttering to himself: 'I do hope you're right, dear boy. I do so hope you're right!'

The doctor wiped his hands on a piece of spare cloth and peered pleasantly over his horn-rimmed glasses at his two visitors. Paul Donavon had graduated twenty years ago from King's College Hospital with great hopes of a distinguished career in medicine. Unfortunately, an addiction to good malt whiskey and pretty legs had brought him two official reprimands from the British Medical Board and knowing full well he would never survive a third without being struck off, he had returned to his native land and a small country practice.

It may not have afforded him the same opportunities as a lucrative Harley Street surgery, but even in this pleasant little village there were benefits for the discerning soul. There was to be had the company of more than one lonely lady, with the added advantage that here, at least, they knew how to keep their mouths tightly shut; and the local brew of Poteen, while not attempting to rival a good malt, did have a certain *ne plus ultra* about it. All in all, the good life could be lived here with very little to disturb his peace and tranquillity.

The girl was a smasher! At forty-five, Paul Donavon could still appreciate the radiant looks of such a woman. He felt more than a little envy at the tall, obviously foreign, man beside her.

'And what can I do for you?' he asked rolling his sleeves down and patting his thin brown hair into shape.

Alana extended her hand and beamed at the doctor. 'I'm Alana Kennedy, doctor, from RTE and this is Tom Mott from CBS News, in New York. We were wondering if you could fill us in a little more on the girl who was found this morning.'

The smile instantly left his face as he motioned them to sit on the old but comfortable couch in his office. 'Ah yes, poor young Betsy. Well now, I don't think there is anything that I can tell you, miss. You see, that will all come under the heading of evidence and, as such, it'll have to wait for the Coroner's Court. I can't be giving it to you first now, can I?'

Mott eased forward slightly. 'We haven't told you *what* we want yet, doctor.'

Doctor Donavon started slightly. 'Ah yes, well . . . of course I assumed you wanted something on the medical evidence side of things.'

He shifted uncomfortably in his chair and Mott sensed intuitively that there was something strange about the death of the girl. 'Why would you assume that, doctor? Surely it's natural for us to want details of the victim's background – the sort of thing a family doctor would know?'

Alana took up the cue. 'Are you saying, doctor, that Betsy's death was . . . well . . . strange? That there was something about it that doesn't quite add up?'

Donavon fidgeted and then suddenly grew angry. 'I'm saying nothing, young lady. I only examined the body superficially. It will be up to the surgeon who performed the post-mortem to make his report to the coroner. At which time you will find out, not before.'

Alana wasn't to be put off. 'You *are* concerned though, aren't you, doctor? Something's on your mind, I can see it in your face. What was so strange about Betsy's death?'

Instantly the hapless doctor stood upright. 'That's enough! I'll thank you to leave now, if you please.'

'So what do you make of all that?' asked Tom when they were once again seated in the MG.

'He was scared, or at least deeply troubled by something, Tom. That much is for sure. You hit it right on the head when you spotted his conclusion that we were after medical evidence. Christ, I'd have probably missed that and steered him onto mundane family history. I feel such an incredible *amateur*!'

Mott squeezed her knee. 'Forget it. You're a cameraman, not a reporter. It takes years to spot an opening like that. Come on, drive over to the pub and I'll regale you with stories of derring-do in the field.'

She laughed happily, the mood dispelled, and did as she was instructed. As the pair walked into the small, spotlessly clean pub, the half-dozen or so locals gathered around the bar stopped talking and turned to scrutinise the new arrivals.

Tom and Alana collected their drinks and sat at a narrow table under one of the two large picture windows in the bar. Alana seemed unaware of the quiet in the room and continued to bubble happily with her lover. Eventually she too noticed the strangeness of the staring faces and looked at Mott for an explanation.

'It's simple really. The girl probably worked in this pub and these men would have known her. They are naturally suspicious of any stranger. Perhaps it would have been better if we hadn't come in.'

As he spoke, a brawny young man pushed himself from the bar and strode over to their table. He planted himself in front of it, thumbs hooked through a broad leather belt, glaring with animosity at the journalist.

'You don't belong here, mister. Who are you?'

Mott returned the level stare and explained who they were and the purpose of their visit to the area. He replaced the glass he had been holding on the table and added, 'Now get your ugly frame away from here!'

The big man shifted his feet slightly and moved towards Mott with a low animal-like growl, hands extended to grip the American by the throat. Tom slid out from behind the table with one fluid movement and, without further argument, drove his clenched fist hard into the big man's stomach. The lad collapsed in an untidy, crumpled heap on the cold stone floor while Mott held out his hand to Alana. 'Time to go, Alana.'

As they left the pub car park, a curtain was pulled slightly back from an upstairs window and a shadowy figure watched them accelerate away. When they were out of sight, the curtain slowly dropped back into place.

Alana drove the sports car at her customary break-neck speed towards Dragha Abbey, taking little-used country lanes which were adorned with trees proclaiming a glorious Irish autumn. Golden-red leaves intermingled with traces of yellow, sharing branches with other leaves that obstinately refused to change from summer green.

The roads were covered with a carpet of crushed fronds which would cause a car to skid given the slightest opportunity. The flashes of sun played through the trees lending an almost surrealistic effect to their mid-afternoon drive.

On leaving the pub they had driven back to the cottage where Tom had changed his clothes and requested that they visit the Abbey. Alana had looked quizzically at him, but the look on his face warned her he was in no mood for questions. She had quickly prepared a sandwich of cold meat and munching the food as they drove he had asked her to fill him in a little more on their filming assignment.

She swung the car onto the opposite side of the road in order to avoid a heavily-laden milk cart pulled by a tired old donkey and told him how Cruachan was the location of an extensive Iron Age settlement and the capital of the King of Connacht. It was from this ancient site that the old kings had set out to perform feats of great daring both within Ireland and across the water in Scotland and how these feats were still remembered to this day by the Irish in legends and folk songs.

She explained to an attentive Mott how the site of

Roiligh na Ríogh, near to the Cave itself, was believed to be the grave of Conn of the Hundred Battles, the greatest of the old kings, and of three queens, including Queen Eire, after whom the country was named.

She confused him briefly by referring to the Cave of Cats, *Owney – grat* in Gaelic, before explaining that this was simply another name for the Cave of Cruachu.

The car swerved to avoid a fallen tree branch and a slight drift of the back wheels was corrected expertly before she continued, concentrating on the cave itself.

'It is thought by the locals to be the entrance to Satan's underworld. He's often called Donn or The Brown One over here, by the way.'

'I know that. Go on,' he urged, leaning with the car as she swung it hard into a left-hand bend.

'Well, this cave is, as I said, thought to be the portal through which the Devil will enter the upper world when he is able to free himself from the chains which bind him in hell. The old Druids believed he would make his attempt on new year's eve, which nowadays falls on October 31st. As they didn't know *which* new year's eve Old Nick would make his break, they instructed that certain rituals should take place *every* year's end throughout eternity to ensure they were present, or their descendants were, at the appointed time.

'Why new year's eve?'

'It's supposed to be the time which belongs neither to the new year nor to the old. A time when the space between the other world and this one is so indistinct that crossing over is an easy matter. Consequently, to the Druids, it's the obvious time for The Brown One to make his move.'

'Okay, so what happens these days on the feast of Samhain?'

Glancing at him with an expression which conveyed

added respect, she said, 'I'm impressed, you know the proper name! Well, not a lot really. As you can imagine the old Druidic rituals have become distorted over the years. There aren't any human sacrifices anymore, obviously, but old Seamus Flynn, he's the local High Priest or whatever of the Druids, does try to keep things respectable by performing incantations he swears are centuries old. The assemblage mix this with modern-day prayers, all designed to exhort God to help keep Satan back.'

Mott smiled to himself. He could just picture the scene. Elderly men and women dressed in bed sheets, fortified with more than a little potent alcohol to keep out the cold, trying to form an orderly circle on a windswept hill late at night with the local lads poking fun. Swilling beer over one another in false bravado ever fearful that it was just possible something devilish *could* come sneaking out of the hole.

'What about the structure of the Cave?'

'Flynn has agreed to take us inside; he knows the tunnels better than anyone. But the entrance clearly shows some human influence had a hand in its layout. As you've seen, the entrance is really just a hole in the ground with a large, flat stone laid across, supported by two boulders. He says there is just enough room to crawl inside and then we'll find the roof and walls are lined with slabs of granite for quite some way into the interior. Apparently, on several of the lintels, someone has carved oghams. They're . . .'

'An early form of alphabet,' he interrupted, 'formed by placing parallel strokes of varying lengths either above or through a single continuous line.'

She flashed a wide grin at him. 'So you're educated as well as good in bed.'

He laughed with her and then asked about the rumours

and stories connected with the Cave. After she had repeated almost verbatim what Harman had already told him, he shook his head in disbelief. 'Surely you don't mean to tell me that people believe this sort of thing – that goblins will snatch you away if they catch you at night on the hill!'

'Don't mock these people,' she said seriously. 'Some of the stories they can tell you about the funny goings-on around the hill would make your hair stand on end, *if* you could get them to talk freely about them.'

Slowing the car and satisfied they had found the right turning, she swung off the road onto a gravel driveway which Mott could see swept in a curving arc for a good quarter of a mile before ducking out of sight behind a thicket of trees. As the wheels of the car crunched their way noisily over the gravel, Tom noted the badly-kept lawns and weed-throttled flower beds and the concrete pads upon which once would have rested wooden park benches.

They cleared the trees and drove towards the main building and Mott now knew this trip had been a waste of time. What was left of the roof hung precariously, threatening to fall into the very guts of the building.

Mott quickly left the car, staring in disappointment at the ruin which confronted him. From his vantage point he could see through what must once have been a magnificent pair of oak doors, swinging eerily to and fro on rusty hinges and which led into the great hall of the building.

Smoke-blackened beams pointed accusing fingers towards the heavens while large black crows wove their way in aimless flight through empty arches and high broken windows. Their cries seemed to echo a lament for all that once was and was now gone into the void of time.

Even as he watched, a black rat darted across a narrow

beam of sunlight and raced up the single remaining support of a burned-out staircase. The windows of the Abbey looked down in gaunt, unspeaking testimony. Weed and grass grew along the façade in wild profusion. Unrestrained, their roots digging into the very heart of the mortar, striving to tear away the large blocks of the structure; determined in their task, the roots would eventually rip the place apart, stone by tortured stone.

As the wind rasped through the dry stone walls he felt suddenly cold and, for just a fleeting moment, he imagined he could hear a shrill and ancient voice, thinly echoing in the thin whispers of the grass.

'What did you expect to find here, Tom?' she asked quietly, sensing his disappointment and at the same time bringing him back to reality.

'A man, or at the very least a clue as to his whereabouts. What do you know about the place?' he asked, pointing at the mass of crumbling grey stone.

She shrugged, searching her memory. 'Not a great deal, I'm afraid. It didn't affect the assignment so I . . .'

He waved an impatient hand to stop her unnecessary explanations. 'Just tell me what you do know, Alana.'

'Built in 1423, I think, and destroyed by fire about two years ago. There was a storm and the building was struck by lightning, early morning before the monks were awake, and as I remember, nobody got out alive. Fifty or sixty killed in the fire. I'm sorry, but that's all I know.'

He looked thoughtfully back at the building and for a moment, as the wind howled through broken tiles, he could almost hear the screams of the human torches. 'No one escaped?'

'As far as I recall, no. It was a very big story at the time.'

He nodded. 'I'll bet it was. Right, let's go.'

She looked at him in surprise. 'Don't you want to have a look around the place now we're here?'

He opened the passenger door and shook his head. 'No point. The man I'm looking for isn't here and, if what you tell me is true, then either I'm mad and I've been talking to a dead man, or the Vatican have been lying through their cassocks. Either way, the answer is back in Rome, not at this burnt-out shell!'

Alana put her hands on her hips and shouted in exasperation across the car, 'What the hell are you talking about? What is going on?'

He waved her into the car with a noncommittal reply. Within seconds they were hurtling back down the gravel driveway, with Alana still demanding to know what Tom had meant. As they turned onto the hard topped road, Mott told her the story from the beginning.

As the sound of the engine died in the distance a large black cat walked casually from the gloomy hallway out onto one of the Abbey steps and stared after the car with cruel eyes. After testing the air with twitching whiskers it left the step and raced across the lawn after them.

CHAPTER SEVEN

At the same time as Alana and Tom were approaching Dragha Abbey, Michael James O'Flahrety finished cleaning the two small candlesticks in St Bernadette's and replaced them on the neat altar with its crisp, white cloth. He then genuflected and walked up the highly polished aisle to make his weekly visit to the elderly couple who occupied one of the thatched cottages behind the parish church.

Father Mike, as he was affectionately known by his parishioners, had awoken this morning shortly after six and for the first time since his evacuation from Dunkirk in a hospital ship, felt no pain whatsoever in his legs. He had slid his legs from the bed and looked down at them with a sense of wonder and thankfulness.

For more than forty years Father Michael had had constant daily reminders of the time when, as a too-young subaltern, he had ordered his squad to attack a farmhouse during the last days of the British Expeditionary Force's abortive attempt to hold France against the onslaught of the German armies which blitzkrieged their way across the fertile land.

Michael had joined the army in 1938, following in the footsteps of many of his ancestors who had fought with, or against, the British, generation after generation gaining military distinctions for the proud family. His parents had been so proud of the young soldier, his father had exhorted him to return with medals and honours in the best tradition of Irish fighting families.

At first, the war had been fun. Like all young men of his generation he had awaited eagerly the first encounter with the enemy. He had written home in couched terms of the regiment's preparations for sailing to France and of his own efforts to get the raw recruits who formed his platoon into shape. His family wrote back reminding him constantly of the heroics of the past O'Flahretys – urging him to try to equal and perhaps even surpass their feats.

Then had come the sailing of the British Expeditionary Force across the Channel to save the world! And the fighting. And the killing. And the cold and mud. The deaths of close comrades, of fellow-officers cut down mercilessly by a more advanced killing machine. The whittling away of his trained squaddies, replaced by even younger men with the benefit of only six short weeks in training camps, unprepared for the real horror of fighting in the fenland country.

All too soon, the British knew the battle was lost. Frantic preparations had to be made to retreat. The word was passed – withdraw to Dunkirk – and, for thousands of younger men, all hopes of glory faded with the order.

For Michael, it was perhaps worse. A sense of utter failure descended on him in those last few days as his platoon, cut off from the rest of the regiment, crept and crawled silently and afraid along ditches and quiet lanes, hoping they would be in time to get safe passage home. A sense more of letting his own family down than of disgrace at the speedy and uncompromising defeat suffered by the nation, began slowly to affect his judgement.

And then, with the seaside port of Dunkirk just two miles away marked by the columns of black smoke winding into the grey sky hour after hour, the young lieutenant saw his opportunity.

They had marched all night knowing that the Germans were racing up behind them, eager to cut off as many of the retreating soldiers as possible. Shortly after dawn he had called a rest under a thick, impenetrable hedgerow so peculiar to this part of the world, in order to scout a small whitewashed farmhouse, positioned on open ground with a perfect view of the surrounding terrain. His training and subsequent field experience had taught him that this location was a perfect spot to mount an observation post or even a machine gun nest. Over-eager troops could, if a reconnoitre was not properly conducted, be cut to pieces in a matter of thirty seconds.

He examined the farmhouse and crumbled barn, evidence, perhaps, of a stray artillery shell, and then swept the hen house and outside toilet with his glasses before returning his attention to the main house, concentrating on the upstairs window. A slight movement! Was it the wind which caused the curtain to shift imperceptibly? Michael trained his glasses on the paneless window for several minutes until, suddenly, he saw an arm protrude slightly as its owner shifted position.

Michael could see the arm, dressed in black with what appeared to be two thin silver stripes on the cuff. *Waffen SS*! The most elite of all German fighting men. Michael felt a thrill run through him at the thought of the opportunity this presented to the platoon – to him.

His corporal objected when Michael outlined his hastily formed plan, pointing out that the tattered platoon could easily take a three-mile detour around the building and thus avoid any action. He also reminded Michael that Waffen SS troops did not travel in twos and threes and that it was highly probable that there was at least platoon strength inside the building. He pressed Michael to abandon the scheme, pleading that, in their present condition, the men simply couldn't take on well-fed, rested troops.

Four of the men were detailed to draw fire from the front while Michael led the remainder to assault the building from the rear and sides. As they moved from cover near the chicken coop, heavy machine guns stationed inside the barn and at the rear ground floor window opened up in a deadly crossfire that scythed its way through the doomed soldiers.

Michael had been the only survivor. He had awoken several hours later in a German field hospital, his legs numb from the several bullets which had smashed into them. He slipped in and out of consciousness, hallucinating in his agony as he thought he saw British soldiers standing with Bren guns over the surgeon as he worked to save the young officer's life.

He had come to full consciousness in a large room filled with the chatter of nurses and the rattle of bedpans. It took him several moments to realise that the voices he was hearing were English and then a soft-spoken doctor explained how he had been rescued by a team of commandos fighting their own way back to their landing craft. They had walked straight into the German hospital compound and walked out with as many British officers as they could carry.

Then had come the Intelligence officers, wanting to know how his platoon had become involved in the action when the intelligent course of action, surely, was to avoid any unnecessary fighting. Hadn't he understood the orders?

He lied to the officers! One of his men had seen the Germans escorting a senior British officer into the house and they had tried to rescue the man. He was a hero – the sole survivor of a brave but futile attempt to help a fellow soldier. Medals were pinned to his pillow; a captaincy;

the adoration of his fellow man. No matter that after the war the young man would be haunted by the screams of the dying soldiers – dying because he had betrayed his own sacred responsibilities to them.

At length, he took Holy Orders in an attempt to cleanse his mind of the dead and their cries. In that he was successful. His soul, at least, would be saved but he never told the army of his deceit. Never returned the medals so proudly encased at his family home. Never lived without the pain in his legs to remind him of his stupidity and his greed.

Until this morning. He felt stronger than he had ever done as he threw wide the windows of his bedroom to let in the early morning sunshine. Today would be a good day. The Lord himself had given him back the strength, had removed the pain. He was forgiven!

He stopped for a brief chat with Mrs Brodie at the gate to the terraced cottage before he walked up the path and into the house announcing himself with a friendly 'It's only me.'

Mr and Mrs Crogan turned and smiled at the priest. Both sat beside the warmth of the fire, Mrs Crogan unable to walk because of the paralysis which had struck her down three years previously and Mr Crogan unwilling to move, save for his twice-daily walk to the village pub. Paddy Crogan nodded towards the untidy kitchen. 'You can make some tea, Father.'

Father Michael patted him affectionately on the shoulder and moved to the kitchen to put the kettle on. He sighed when he saw the sink full of dirty crockery. Old Crogan would never fend for himself so long as one of the Craghan ladies kept coming in to do little things for the couple. Michael knew that Crogan took advantage of them but, as he also realised, the ladies of the village liked to feel that they were doing some good.

He made the tea and placed the unsliced loaf on a breadboard and carried it into the living room. Then he returned to the kitchen and found the sharp bread knife, butter and jam and three reasonably clean plates and placed these on the table behind the old man.

As he cut the bread he talked of the village events that the old woman loved to hear about, mixing it with a little harmless gossip. Then he handed the woman a mug of hot tea and a slice of buttered bread with a healthy portion of jam, giving the same to her husband.

Crogan took a greedy bite of the bread and stopped in mid-chew as he felt something draw across his throat. Biddy Crogan stared uncomprehendingly at the thin red line stretching from her husband's left ear right the way round to his right. Her mouth gaped open as the line widened with the force of separated neck muscles and his arteries spurted deep crimson blood into the fire.

She looked up at the priest with horror-struck eyes, unable to accept what they told her, as the glinting knife in his hand moved towards her, a strange look on his face and an incredible brightness radiating from his eyes – eyes which had looked so kindly down upon her with such love in the past. Before she thought to scream, Father Michael grabbed her hair and wrenched her head painfully backwards to expose her slack-skinned neck. Hot, foul breath washed over her in sickening waves. He spat in her face and then cut her throat.

Afterwards, he washed the dishes and restoked the fire before returning to his church. He walked down the aisle, so lovingly polished by a succession of devout villagers and stood in front of the neat altar, with the two silver candlesticks bought for the church after months of saving by the parishioners.

He took off his trousers, urinated over the marble and once his bladder was empty he climbed onto the crisp, white cloth and defecated there. Then he wiped his anus with pieces of communion bread taken from the chalice inside the tabernacle.

At last, satisfied with his work, he retrieved the length of rope from behind the front pew where he had hidden it earlier, and threw one end over the crossbeam just above the pulpit. Then he climbed onto the pulpit's rail and noosed the rope around his neck before anchoring the other end to the railing.

As he jumped the demon left his body and Father Michael James O'Flahrety knew he was condemned to eternal damnation.

Margaret Brodie waved a cheery farewell to Father Michael and carried on her way to the butcher's shop. She always felt a slight thrill when she was near the priest as he reminded her so much of Paul Clancy.

She often looked at Father Michael while he was saying Mass on Sunday or thundering dire predictions from the pulpit and imagined this was how Clancy would have looked now: tall, strong with a kind face and manner, attentive and caring. She hated Sundays because, after Mass, she would return to the large, empty house on the edge of the village and spend the rest of the day dreaming about those far-off days when she was a very desirable seventeen-year-old.

Her family were Roscommon people, reasonably well off, as her widowed father had worked hard at the haberdashery shop he had opened in Frenchpark. Over the years first one shop and then another had been bought and through diligence and industry the family had become the proud owners of no less than twelve shops spread throughout the South.

It was inevitable that her father would want to grow

even richer. She remembered still her father arriving home later than usual one afternoon and announcing that the family were now entering the manufacturing business, in partnership with a powerful family from nearby Boyle. The Clancys had needed extra manufacturing space for their textile concerns and Margaret's father had seen a heaven-sent opportunity to co-purchase a mill, thus allowing him to become his own supplier.

The two families had met at the Clancy mansion the following Saturday and, as soon as Margaret had set eyes on Paul, she knew they would be lovers. Paul was articulate and well mannered with just a hint of haughtiness. Three years older than she, he was experienced in the ways of the world and in the ways of male–female relationships.

Paul, in turn, was delighted with the young country girl's innocent ways, often driving over to Craghan to visit her for picnics on the river, or going together into Dublin to see the latest film at the old Roxy. He talked often about leaving Ireland to enlist in a British regiment in order that he could 'get a crack at the Huns before they land in Ireland'.

On these occasions she would implore him to stay in neutral Ireland, unable to understand why he would want to risk his life in a war which didn't concern them. Then he would laugh merrily and pull her to him, smothering her mouth with warm, passionate kisses.

They had known each other barely a year when she found she was pregnant. She tortured herself for days before telling Paul and he reacted in a way she would never have thought possible. Her gentle, sensitive lover started to rant and rage, telling her it was all her fault and the disgrace would be intolerable to his family.

Dumbfounded, she had listened to his hastily conceived plan. She would have an abortion! He knew a man at

Dublin University, who knew a man, who knew where it could be done. He would make all the arrangements.

As though in a dream, the following Saturday morning she stepped into his new Morris and drove with him to Dublin to see the abortionist. Unwilling, yet afraid of losing Paul, she was led into the dirty room where the life growing inside her was murdered.

Days later she received a letter from Paul telling her of his decision to go to war. Six months later he was dead, killed by a German sniper in an obscure desert town. Margaret was left alone to bear the deep sense of guilt and shame.

By the end of the war, her father had died of a heart attack brought on by overwork. Margaret plunged herself into the dizzy world of commerce, taking the small family concern from its back-street image into the vibrant world of modern-day salesmanship. She expanded, growing with a ruthlessness which surprised all who knew her, unaware that Margaret's passionate immersion into business was a shield against her overriding conviction that she had committed a cardinal sin by her liaison, out of wedlock, with Paul Clancy, hideously compounded by her complicity in the murder of an innocent, unbaptised soul.

She had never married. Indeed, after Paul there had never been any other man to explore the delights of her body. What she did have was her fantasies within the privacy of her bedroom, fantasies which brought other pressures and longings that screamed for release – to be freed only by her own hand as she lay in the warmth, stroking and penetrating herself in furtive moments of pleasure.

Lately she had started to fantasise about the priest, or about the strong healthy young butcher with his red, hard hands. She would lie in bed listening to the wind touching the eaves, the house creaking in its comforting way, imagining that the bolster beside her was the young body of the meat cutter and that it was his hands which now massaged her, his rough finger now penetrating.

Margaret arrived at the clean, white shop and glanced in the window at the pig's head, neatly arranged with pork chops spread out at either side laced with sprigs of parsley to add just the right touch of colour, before stepping onto the comforting sawdust inside.

Twoomey Halloran stepped forward, a broad grin on his face, his shirt unbuttoned to the slim waist. His muscular chest rose and fell with his easy breathing and Margaret felt a thrill at the sight as her brain flashed a momentary image of him lying on top of her, thrusting with all his might.

'Good afternoon, Miss Brodie, I was just going to lunch, but I'll take care of you first. What can I do for you?'

Smiling, she nodded towards the pig's head. 'I'd like some nice chops, two I think, and a piece of sirloin, please.'

Swiftly he wrapped the chops and picked up a large piece of sirloin. He looked at it for a second, wrinkled his nose and threw it back onto the plastic tray. 'I don't think that's good enough for you, Miss Brodie. Tell you what, drop the catch on the door and come into the preparation room – I've got just the thing for you!'

She looked at him curiously. 'The catch . . . ?'

Twoomey nodded. 'Aye, the catch. I want to be away for me dinner as soon as I've served you. I've been trying this last half hour since.'

She did as she was bid and walked after him into the rear of the shop. She had never been in this part before and she glanced around with the curiosity one trader has for another's business. She saw with approval the clean instruments hanging in their proper place and the meat blocks scrubbed as clean as a pin. The shop was kept with a pride one has for one's profession and she turned to compliment Twoomey on his care and attention.

The words froze in Margaret's throat as she saw the strange expression on the man's face. 'Why are you looking at me like that, Twoomey?'

Without replying, the butcher walked towards her, his chest rising and falling and Margaret felt an expectant thrill course through her. Was it possible? She felt his strong hands on her shoulders, pushing down with a strength she had only dreamed of. Her knees buckled and she crumpled on the floor, Twoomey slowly dropping on top of her.

Margaret felt the pounding in her blood and she knew she was wet. Very wet. In her imagination she had often dreamt of being taken this way, raped by a man as virile and strong as Twoomey, legs forced apart and his solid organ ramming its way into her. She struggled. She had to show a pretence of fighting, couldn't let him think she had wanted this for so long. Needed it! Oh God, she thought in mounting excitement, as his hands ran over her breasts, he's going to rape me until it hurts . . .

The hard, red hands ran over her breasts and squeezed them painfully and she felt the pure, unbridled ecstasy of a man's hands on her body after all these lonely years. She shifted her body a little as though she were struggling, but the real purpose was to allow him to jam his leg between hers and make it easier for him to get his hand between her thighs.

Those hands! Pressing and kneading her breasts and now travelling up her throat and stroking her. She wished he would get to it and she raised herself slightly in a movement which could be construed as further, weak attempts at escape. She pressed against his groin, opening her eyes in wide-eyed astonishment at the hardness in his trousers. It had been so long she had forgotten what it was really like!

She wanted to say to him: 'Now! Do it now. Fuck me with all your strength. Again and again and again. Ram it into me!' Instead she looked at Twoomey in puzzlement as his rough hands tightened about her throat and squeezed. 'Oh God,' her mind screamed, 'he's not going to rape me, he's going to kill me!'

Margaret Brodie kicked out with a force dissipated only by his leg jamming between hers and she struggled and fought as those hands tightened inexorably. He was killing her slowly, enjoying every moment of the excitement of doing so. As she slipped into unconsciousness, the last sight Margaret Brodie had was of the butcher drooling over her, his eyes shining brighter than she would have thought possible.

Later that afternoon, the Garda officer, Patrick, was roused from his afternoon nap by a hysterical woman calling from outside Twoomey's shop. He couldn't make head nor tail of the garbled message and, after a moment, he instructed her to wait there and he drove over to Craghan to see what all the trouble was about.

A small crowd was gathered around the shop and he elbowed his way through, cursing as he did so, to the window.

He was dumbstruck by the sight which confronted him and he crossed himself before racing back to the car to call headquarters.

All the while, the head of Margaret Brodie stared impassively from the window display, where she now took pride of place over the pig's head.

In Dublin, in a cluttered little office, reached by way of a dirty alleyway off O'Connell Street, a telephone jangled insistently. After a while, the Duty Officer walked to the desk and spoke a single 'yes' into the mouthpiece. He listened to the caller without speaking, but made hurried notes on the pad beside the instrument. He asked a few questions and then, satisfied, replaced the receiver in its cradle without a thank you and walked hurriedly from the room to another, larger room along the corridor.

He pushed open the office door without knocking and Colonel Ambrose looked up. 'It's started, sir,' said the Duty Officer handing him the notepad.

Ambrose read it quickly and reached for his own telephone which was routed through the Security Service's own switchboard. He instructed the operator to obtain a Rome number for him and while he waited for the connection he covered the mouthpiece and spoke rapidly to the officer.

'Seal the village off as per planned. No through traffic, no calls in or out unless they go through our own switchboard. Seal it off tight and make sure the Restricted Item notices go out to the press on the story. If anybody asks, tell 'em we've discovered an enormous arms cache in the village. Okay?'

The officer nodded and turned from the room as Colonel Ambrose's call came and he heard the start of the conversation before the office door closed. 'Monsignor? This is Amb . . .'

Colonel Ambrose stretched languidly in front of the fire and felt more relaxed than he had done for several hours. He had raced to the butcher's shop in Craghan as soon as he had completed the call to Rome and, even for someone well used to the savagery of man, he had been appalled at what he had seen.

Police officers had cordoned off the pavement in front of

the shop and as he alighted from the Ford an expectant buzz had run through the assembled villagers. They would, he reasoned, assume him to be a murder squad detective sent from the city. The head remained in the window, awaiting the arrival of the official police photography team, although thankfully one of the officers had had the intelligence to cover it with a gauze cloth.

Ambrose walked inside and reached into the window, lifting one corner of the material. He studied the head, noting the precision with which it had been severed, before replacing the rag and allowing himself to be led into the rear by the police inspector.

The meat locker stood open and it took Ambrose several seconds to comprehend that the fresh, unfrozen meat hanging in rows was all that remained of the unfortunate woman. Two arms hung neatly skewered beside two legs and the torso had been cut lengthways to resemble two sides of beef awaiting purchase.

The inspector had indicated the meat mincer warranted closer scrutiny and Ambrose had seen piles of meat standing ready in orderly trays, waiting to be fed through the cutters. There was little doubt these would prove to be human organs and intestines once they were sent to the forensic laboratory.

Following his inspection, Ambrose was led to the upper portion which contained the living quarters. It was here that they had located Twoomey.

On the floor of the living room, untidy as befitted a bachelor, they found the ordered pile of fingers from his left hand and ten white toes which the maniac had evidently chopped off with a meat cleaver before he had stepped from the chair, allowing the meat hook to penetrate through his jaw. The look of anguish etched in the face told Ambrose that the man must have died a slow, excruciatingly painful death.

Within the hour they had found the bodies of the Crogans and Father Michael. Ambrose felt the stabbing anguish of fear – a fear born of the knowledge that he could do little to stop the madness; that he, like so many others, was simply a pawn, helpless and useless in a game he didn't understand and, until coming to this otherwise peaceful village, hadn't really believed.

Piecing together the facts of the case after seeing both the bodies of the priest and the elderly couple, he came to his own conclusions regarding the happenings here. He listened with apparent agreement as the inspector postulated that Twoomey had been Betsy's rapist and killer; had murdered the elderly couple probably after delivering something to them; murdered the priest who had probably witnessed Twoomey entering the house and then murdered Miss Brodie before taking his own life.

The inspector pronounced himself content with the theory and looked to the assembled officers for contradictory evidence. There was none forthcoming, and Ambrose had to admit that it was feasible that one man could murder five times. Twoomey would be the logical suspect, particularly as a dismembered corpse had been found in his shop.

But the look on Twoomey's dead face told him that it just wasn't so. The look was one of sudden realisation, anger, terror. Hope, even, of what? Salvation? Yes, that had been there too. It wasn't . . . most certainly wasn't . . . the face of a maniac murderer who had taken his own life. Maniacs didn't commit suicide. They went on until they were stopped.

As he left the shop he had glanced towards the pub and stared at the small window on the second floor. The curtain moved slightly to indicate he was there and Ambrose felt a flush of deep resentment welling inside him. He climbed back into the car, instructing the driver to take him to the little cottage on the edge of the village. It was time he met this Tom Mott – time to face the worst enemy he had ever encountered in his life.

He rubbed his hands in front of the fire appreciatively and then returned his attention to the two men as Alana entered from the kitchen bearing a tray laden with coffee and biscuits.

'So, Mr Doyle, you and Miss Kennedy here work for RTE but you're on loan to CBS for the purpose of shooting a documentary. Is that right?'

Doyle nodded. He had been shocked to see the Colonel standing at the doorway when he had gone to answer the bell, but it took only a furtive grimace from the security man to tell Doyle they were not to give any indication of knowing each other.

'That's right. It's not uncommon for staff who are on contract to one network to be loaned to another if workloads permit.'

Ambrose nodded. He already knew all this, of course, but he felt it advisable to start at the beginning rather than risk this Mott character grasping the fact that he was aware of their every move.

Doyle had been right about Mott, he thought as he studied the American. He was a tough-looking man in a highly competent way. The type of man you wanted to have on your side when the going got rough. Above all, Ambrose could sense the extreme confidence emanating from him.

'And you, Mr Mott, perhaps you could tell me what this story is all about?'

Mott gave their visitor a brief synopsis, aware that as he spoke Ambrose's eyes never left Alana, evidently appreciative of her lithe form. When he had concluded, the officer politely questioned the girl as to their whereabouts that afternoon.

Ambrose asked a few further routine questions and then, after thanking them for their time, and coffee, announced himself satisfied. As he stood to go, Mott demanded to know why they had been subjected to questioning. Ambrose buttoned his overcoat and slipped on his gloves carefully and answered.

'You obviously haven't heard that there has been a rather nasty incident in the village today. The Garda think the local butcher went off his head and murdered an elderly couple, a spinster and the parish priest before committing suicide. Very nasty business. We just wanted to see if you knew anything.'

Alana looked both horrified and professionally interested. 'Betsy, was she . . . ?'

'Killed by the same man? Yes, it looks that way. Well, once again, many thanks and I'm sorry to have disturbed you. Goodnight.'

As the car sped away from the cottage Ambrose hoped that Doyle hadn't missed his hint about the Garda *thinking* it was the butcher. Ambrose was content to let the civil police carry on in their ignorance, but it could be fatal for Doyle if he relaxed his guard. As he reached the crossroads he talked rapidly into his hand microphone to police headquarters and ordered the lifting of the restrictions around the village. Let things take their allotted course, he muttered to himself as his driver put his foot down and raced back towards Dublin.

CHAPTER EIGHT

'Hey, mister, I'd like a word with you!'

Tom shifted slightly on the bar stool and tensed when he saw the speaker was the man whom he had punched only the week before in this very pub. The stockily-built farm labourer towered above him and he resigned himself to a repeat of last week's unpleasantness.

In the ensuing time since the spate of murders the American had kept his two-man team busy with the filming of the documentary. They had interviewed Seamus Flynn three times and were satisfied with his contribution only after the third filming when the man had relaxed in front of the unaccustomed cameras long enough to tell his story with lucidity and not a little Irish charm and humour.

The village had buzzed for a few days with varying accounts and explanations as to why the butcher had gone off his head. But then the talk had subsided, finally receding altogether once the inquest had been held in Frenchpark. The subject became closed among the close-knit villagers who preferred to forget that such an incident could ever have happened in their community. The general consensus was that, as the butcher was a relative newcomer to the village, it was hardly surprising that he had bad blood in his veins.

Seamus himself felt it had to be the influence of the approaching Samhain which had caused the trouble and he rambled at great length as he escorted the camera team through the maze of tunnels at the Cave of Cruachu that afternoon.

It had been just as Alana had said. The opening was just wide enough for them to slip through, one at a time and, once past the entrance, they had been able to stand upright in the tunnel. Alana flipped on her camera lights and the scene that appeared was, to Tom at least, quite breathtaking. For as far as the powerful lights threw their beam, heavy stone blocks lined the route and covered the roof of the tunnel. The impression was of having entered a lovingly prepared tomb.

After several hundred yards, the slabbed walls and roof petered out and they entered a network of un-shored tunnels which meandered under and through the surrounding hillside. Seamus explained, as he moved ahead of them, that many of the tunnels had been formed naturally by long-expired underground streams, or by fissures separating the rocks at the time of the earth's upheaval, millions of years ago. Yet others bore the distinctive marks of having been hewn by hand-wielded tools, evidence of the importance of the area to early miners seeking metal in the earth for weaponry.

Seamus walked about the labyrinthine tunnels with a familiarity and ease born of years of exploration and pointed out old rock falls giving the dates when they had slid from the roof, or tunnels into which one person or another had wandered never to be seen again. Alana was intrigued to learn that there had been several such cases of lost explorers who had been unable to find their way back to the surface. Somewhere in the dark depths of the cave lay, who knew how many, lost souls. Death must have been preceded by madness as light, food and water were finally exhausted.

At last, the old man stopped and turned to face the trio who were dutifully following him. 'This is as far as we can go,' he had said. 'I don't know the way past this point and I'm not about to risk us getting lost.'

They backtracked to the surface and Alana pronounced herself content with the footage she had obtained from their expedition. The sky lay heavy and leaden as they returned to the station wagon. Seamus glanced upwards, a frown crossing his weather-beaten face. 'There's something terrible ominous about the sky these last few days,' he said to no one in particular, as Doyle drove down the hill towards the warmth of the pub in Craghan.

Mott knew what the old man meant. For the past week the weather had become dull and threatening as though mustering itself for a tremendous onslaught over the region.

Dark, grey clouds shifted and wheeled about the sky, gathering together like sheep being herded into pens. The clouds had been building up until they formed a solid, impenetrable mass of blackness which blocked out any trace of autumn sun, hanging like an evil mantle over the village and surrounding countryside. There was little wind around to disperse the cloud bank and the weather men on the local station muttered incessantly about freak inversions trapping the cloud bank over County Roscommon.

It became an irritant to the villagers. This heaviness brought with it an oppression of spirit reflected in the faces of the normally light-hearted residents. And the humidity! Mott had been mildly surprised that such humid conditions could exist this far inland.

At first, the locals had laughed about the freak weather, joked that when it came the storm would wash away half the county. But after seven days and as many sleepless nights the joking had worn thin and now only a rare glance at the threatening heavens was given as they went silently about their business.

'I said I'd like a word with you!'

The American sighed as the flat, toneless statement was repeated. They had entered the pub on the insistence of Flynn, who felt he deserved a good drink for acting as guide. This time their entry had been greeted with, if not friendly nods, at least courteous ones.

'What can I do for you, pal?' replied Mott evenly, preparing to dodge the expected blow.

The brawny Irishman stuck out a hand which looked as if it were used for crushing walnuts. 'I wanted to apologise for me behaviour towards you and the lady the other day. Me mind must have been astray, is all,' he said with a shamefaced grin.

Mott relaxed and shook the hand. 'Understandable, will you have a drink with me?'

The grin was replaced with a solemn look as befitted a man who had just established peace. 'I will that, sir, and thank you for your understanding. I'll have a whiskey.'

The mood in the bar visibly relaxed and the men returned to the duty of drinking. Tom and the brawny lad toasted each other before draining their glasses in one swallow. The lad patted Mott on the back and returned to his own cronies and Seamus chuckled appreciatively.

'Ah now, that's a sight worth staying alive for, so it is. Paddy there is a bloody tough customer and he must think you're a hell of a man to want to shake your hand like that. The punch you gave him must have knocked him for six!'

Alana moved a little closer to Tom and said: 'It was, Seamus. Tom flattened him with one punch to the belly.'

Doyle sullenly waved to the barman to refill their glasses and Seamus cradled the large whiskey gratefully, savouring every drop of the malt as it wound its smooth way to his stomach.

They turned as one at the sound of the door opening

and a young man entered. After a moment's hesitation he walked to the bar and spoke to the landlord in an obviously English accent.

'Excuse me, I'm on my way north with my wife and kid and I don't think we can make the next camp site before dark. Can you tell me if there's anywhere around here where we can park the caravan or get rooms for the night?'

The landlord looked thoughtful for a moment and then shook his head. 'No, sir, I don't think there is. Maybe you'd be better pushing on to Boyle, it's not that far.'

The man seemed dejected. 'Haven't you got rooms you could let me have for one night? One room would do!'

The man shook his head adamantly. 'No, sir, I don't do Bed and Breakfast at all. Sorry!' and with that he moved away to serve at the far end of the bar.

Seamus looked at the landlord, a slight glimmer of distaste flickered across his face, before turning to the Englishman. 'I've got a field you can park your caravan in, mister. Keep going through the village until you pass a row of pink-painted cottages on your left. Turn in at the five-bar gate, about half a mile past on the right. You'll see a clump of trees, park in there. If you want milk or anything like that, go to the house along the little path and see me missus.'

After the Englishman had left, Seamus drained his drink and called for another round which he let Tom pay for. As the barman poured them, Seamus leaned across the bar. 'Tell me now, Paddy, why'd you tell that young feller that you didn't do the Bed and Breakfast when you know full well you do?'

'You mind your own business, Seamus,' retorted the surly landlord.

'I will that, Paddy, but I'm still curious as to why you

didn't want to help the young lad. That's not like you at all.'

Paddy slammed the glasses down with more force than necessary. 'I'm full up if it's any of your business.'

Seamus shook his head. 'Sure and you're not. You only have the queer feller staying with you in the front room. You've lots of space up there.'

A look as black as the sky outside came over the publican and he walked away without further words while Seamus looked after him.

'If the guy says he's full up then he must be full,' said Mott, unsure why it mattered to the old man.

Seamus turned. 'But he's not. My missus does the cleaning here for him and she says he's only got the one staying. Same one as has been here for the past couple of weeks. A real strange cove, so he is. Never leaves his room except to go to the toilet. Takes all his meals up there, so he does.'

Mott cared little about the landlord's mysterious guest and turned the conversation back to the filming. He intended to complete any outstanding sequences, including the festivities on the evening of the 31st, and leave the village on the 1st of November for Rome.

The one item not yet obtained was film of the villagers' preparations for the festival. In past years the entire community had lent a hand in decorating the streets and flint cottages with bunting and flowers. This year, however, it seemed as though the spirit had been drained from them as they were unable to generate any enthusiasm for what had traditionally been as big an excuse for a party as the Harvest Festival. Seamus was understandably upset that the festival he'd come to think of as his special responsibility was being so ignored by the parish.

Eventually, after Seamus had imbibed liberally, they had a solid series of scenes planned for the festival itself.

They would shoot the actual torchlight procession of nine Druids out of the village, along the road and up the hillside. Seamus pointed out locations on Doyle's ordnance survey map where he felt it would be best to place the camera and sound-recording equipment. Once at the cave itself, Mott realised he would have to allow Alana free rein to decide positioning. Seamus was honest enough to admit that quite often the ritual dissolved rapidly through a combination of drink and natural reluctance by the participants to be too near the cave on this special night.

They dropped Flynn off at his cottage before, worn out and slightly tipsy, they returned to their own accommodation. Doyle immediately excused himself and went to his room. As he climbed the stairs Mott watched him, listening for the sound of his door closing. He turned to Alana, drawing her towards him.

'Miserable bastard, isn't he?' he said while smothering her neck with light kisses.

Alana responded, nibbling at his ear lobe hungrily. 'Take no notice of Doyle. I think he's jealous!'

'Does he have cause to be?' Mott's hand ran lightly over her firm breasts and he felt the growing erection bursting against his trousers.

'Don't ask,' she replied softly.

They kissed each other passionately and then she suddenly pulled away from him. 'I'll fix some coffee to take to bed. You go on upstairs.'

He clicked on the bedroom light, stripped off his jacket and hung it on the hook behind the wooden door. Picking up a corner of the coverlet, he pulled it out from under the pillows.

Adnan Hourani's document-case lay there, carefully placed beneath it!

He stared, not touching it, almost not breathing, in

utter bewilderment at the reappearance of the lost case. The dropping of the door latch brought him back to his senses and he turned towards Alana.

'It's the case. The one stolen from my room in Italy!'

Moving to his side she too stared down at the object as if she half-expected it to leap off the bed. Her hand slipped through his arm and she spoke in a hoarse whisper. 'Is the parchment thing inside?'

He cursed himself. So shocked at seeing the case in the bed, he had not thought to open it to see if the priceless manuscript was also there. Mott sat on the edge of the bed, rapidly untied the red silk ribbons and opened the case. He folded back the tissue paper and let his breath out slowly. The parchment was intact!

'Tom . . . I don't understand what's happening. You say this thing was stolen from you in Rome, yet here it is in your bed! How can that happen?'

Relacing the ribbons, he sat for a moment with the case cradled in his hands. 'I don't know, Alana, I honestly don't. It seems that someone is playing a game, or . . .'

'Or what?'

'Well, it's crazy I know, but it's almost as though it were a . . . a . . . warning or a message.'

'*A what?*'

He quieted her. 'Look at it rationally. This manuscript was stolen from my hotel room – it's valuable, priceless perhaps – and then it turns up in my room, in my bed, way over here in Ireland! Now that can't be because the thieves had a change of heart, can it, so there has to be another reason and the only one I can come up with is that it's either a message or a warning of some kind. But what, God only knows.'

He crossed to the small window and stared out into the black night, searching for an answer in the uncompromising darkness. Once again the parchment had plunged him into deep mystery. He had been convinced the answer to its loss lay back at the Vatican, but now, with the parchment returned, it was clear that straightforward theft had not been the motive behind its original disappearance.

But that didn't explain the enigma surrounding Father Falangi, nor did it tell him who had returned the document. Suddenly he remembered the odd stranger who had taken a room at the pub. Could there be a link between his arrival in the village and the return of Hourani's parchment? He knew then he had to meet the man.

'I'm going out,' he said reaching for his check jacket. 'Don't wait up and don't let anybody in. I don't want to lose it again!'

He had left the room before she could answer and it took her several time-consuming moments to fathom just what he'd said. She raced to the top of the stairs and called after him: 'Tom? Tom!' The click of the front door closing was the only reply. She returned to the bedroom, sat on the bed, drawing her knees up and clasping them with her hands, her eyes not leaving the strange parchment.

Mike Banks swore, kicking out at the lump of wood which lay on the path. Rain dripped incessantly from his flat cap and despite all his precautions, found its way easily between the pulled-up collar of his raincoat and the cold skin of his neck to run unhindered down his back. He was cold, hungry, tired and bloody pissed-off!

They had left Dublin too late that afternoon to make the camp site near Boyle and had it not been for the friendly farmer at the pub allowing them to use his field for the night, he would really have lost his temper with his wife. And then the rain had started – just as he set off for the farmhouse!

He had warned Mary they shouldn't leave it too late, but she had insisted on 'doing' Dublin properly. He nearly screamed with rage after they had lost their way for the fourth time as a result of his wife's pathetic attempts to navigate.

It wouldn't have been so bad, he thought, as he stepped blindly into another rain-filled hole, if this hadn't been the first holiday they had been able to afford since they married nine years ago. 'Nine bloody years of grafting,' he muttered again, 'and I end up in a friggin' cow field with rain pissing down my bleedin' neck!'

A noise to the right caused him to halt for a moment before walking on. It came again, louder, a crashing noise as though something were thrashing its way through the undergrowth towards him. He tried to peer through the gloom, but couldn't see a thing. Then the odour reached him. Pungent and sweet, like fish left on the quayside in a hot sun. He wrinkled his nose and waved a hand in front of him to dispel the foulness and then he heard the rasping pant.

'Fuck this,' he muttered and turned away, walking a little quicker than before towards the welcoming light of the farmhouse where he had been informed he could obtain milk.

His trip proved successful, but a sense of unease lingered. Instead of using the pathway on his return to the caravan, Banks kept to the main road as far as the five-bar gate which marked the entrance to the field. Although there were no lights on the highway, the passing cars, infrequent though they were, did reassure him, and he welcomed the hardness of the road beneath his feet. As he pushed open the gate and strode quickly across the field, the glow from the caravan windows and the aroma of cooking sausages did much to dispel his fears. It was probably, after all, only a bloody cow, he thought, as he reached the steps to the Bluebird.

Banks knew instantly that something was wrong. That smell was here, covering the very ground upon which the caravan stood. The door handle felt sticky and he removed his hand and sniffed at it, recoiling instantly at the foulness of the smell. 'Mary! Jenny!' he shouted, wrenching open the door and stepping inside.

The horror left him speechless as he strove to take in the sight before him: tables and fitted cupboards smashed to pieces; clothes flung about, mixed with broken pieces of pottery. His daughter, Jennifer, lay on her back, head dangling in a small stainless steel sink, eyes wide and staring, her dress ripped from her young, child's body. There was blood on her, violent smears across her thighs and stomach, testimony to a brutal rape.

He found his wife on the floor, her naked body bruised and broken. In vain he caressed the lacerations, hoping to heal them, to go back in time, to undo this unthinkable savagery. She groaned slightly and Banks cradled her in his strong arms, lifting her gently from the floor.

The movement released a blood clot. With a gurgling rush, hot sticky blood intermingled with Mary's intestines and flooded from her vagina, washing over his outstretched foot. He screamed loudly and put his hand on her to stem the bleeding. Banks saw with uncomprehending eyes that her vagina had been split right past her anus and he knew his wife too was beyond help. He was vaguely aware of the door to the caravan opening and, as his wife grew limp and died, he looked up at the help which had come too late.

As he did so, the odour of rotting fish moved towards him. The last sight Mike Banks ever had was a great claw reaching down and hooking itself under his breast plate just before the cacodemon tore out his heart.

Tom ducked into the shadows and waited impatiently while a man finished urinating drunkenly against the outside wall at the rear of the pub. He shook himself a couple of times and then, with great difficulty, re-zipped his trousers to stand rigid against the wall, a look of extreme effort on his face. The belch came first, then a long fart and finally the drunk staggered happily back through the rear door into the bar.

The journalist looked around and followed. He had discounted the idea of approaching the innkeeper to ask directly if he could see his guest. He would have sounded demented – 'Hello, I'd like to see the man who's staying here. I don't know who he is.'

He had walked to the village, notwithstanding the rain. Having gazed up at the darkened front room he then slipped around the back and waited for nearly an hour for the kitchen light to go out. Without a raincoat he had quickly become drenched and the fact that the oppressive weather had finally broken did little to lighten his mood. The kitchen light shone relentlessly on.

Finally he had decided he would have to risk moving through the lit kitchen to the stairs and had started towards the back door. Then the drunk had come staggering through. Mott had been forced to step backwards, one foot becoming submerged in a deep muddy puddle.

Now, he could try again. Stealthily he opened the door a fraction and peered through the crack. The bar was full of happy drinkers and the sound of a fiddle swam through the air. He should be able to make it. The gathering would be more intent on what was happening in the bar than on looking at him. He slipped through the door and walked straight ahead, four steps, to the stairs. He was now out of sight of the customers. His only risk was bumping into someone upstairs. Mott elected to climb swiftly up the extreme edge of the staircase to avoid hitting any squeaky treads. Within moments he was standing on the landing. There were six doors to choose from and, quickly getting his bearings, he discounted two. They would look out over the rear of the building.

He wished he could turn the light on but it was too risky. Should the landlord go into the downstairs kitchen he would definitely see it. If possible, he wanted to leave the same way he had arrived – quietly.

Mott put an ear to the first door on the left and listened. All was quiet. Stealthily he turned the handle and eased open the door. It was a toilet. He listened at the next, again opening the door when the stillness indicated another empty room. A bathroom.

Two doors remained. He moved towards the brown-painted one and pressed his ear to the door. The faint sounds of a police siren reached him – a television programme. This was probably the lounge. With extreme care he opened the door and peeked through. A young man was laboriously making love to a teenage girl while she watched Starsky and Hutch, his naked backside rising and falling as he competed against her TV idols. Mott allowed himself a smile as he gently closed the door, moving to the fourth.

This proved to be a bedroom and from the mixture of male and female clothing scattered untidily about he reasoned the room belonged to the couple who owned the pub.

He quickly checked the remaining two rooms overlooking the rear just to ensure they were empty. One was decorated with pin-up posters of the latest pop groups, obviously the young girl's, and the other proved to be a spare bedroom, stripped down and awaiting customers.

Mott moved back to the stairs and only then did he notice the three short steps on the opposite side, leading to a sub-landing. He could see that off this was one single door. And it overlooked the street.

From below he heard the sound of the last orders bell and knew his time was fast running out. He hurried up the short flight and tapped once on the door before turning the handle and walking inside.

It was empty. He flipped the wall light switch and looked around with a sense of despondency. On the journey from the cottage he had convinced himself that the mysterious lodger had something to do with Hourani's manuscript, perhaps having waited patiently for the right moment to slip the folder back into Mott's possession.

But this room bore no trace of recent occupancy. The bed was stripped and the mattress rolled down to the foot of the bed, bare springs showing that, at best, it would afford an uncomfortable night's rest. He moved to the wardrobe, opened it, scanned the interior and closed the door, moving to the three-drawer bureau. It too was empty, save for ample traces of fluff. Similarly the bedside table revealed nothing as to the last occupant of this damp-smelling room.

'What the hell are you doing here?'

Mott had been about to reach for the piece of paper in the wastebasket when the harsh voice made him whirl around. The landlord blocked the doorway to the room, a scowl creasing his rugged face.

'I was looking for the toilet, I got lost,' explained Mott glibly.

'It's outside, not up here. Now on your way.'

Mott shrugged indifferently and turned from the room ahead of the landlord. When they reached the bottom of the stairs the publican jerked a thumb towards the back door. 'It's out that way, mister, and you're a liar. You left hours ago. If you come back I'll break your head. Understand what I'm saying to you?'

Mott nodded and stepped back out into the rain wishing he had been able to grab the piece of paper in the garbage bin. He was sure it had been an Alitalia airline ticket!

Alana moved about the kitchen preparing a late snack for herself. She had woken a short time ago, chilled and cramped on top of Tom's bed, disturbed by the pealing clatter of thunder. The rain hammered with ferocity against the small window panes, the room illuminated by frequent flashes of lightning. The weather had finally broken and for that she was grateful.

She had watched the rivulets of water course their way down the greasy glass of the bedroom window, trying to see through the darkness, hoping vainly to catch sight of Tom hurrying back. Alana knew her lover hadn't returned. Lately, she had been able to sense his presence as though some built in radar was able to tune itself to him, telling her at all times how he felt and when he wanted her.

Turning away from the depressing sight beyond the window she had slipped into the housecoat Aunt Megan had bought her last Christmas and left the room. If nothing else, she had decided, Tom would at least have a pot of hot coffee waiting for him on his return.

As she poured herself a cup a noise from outside startled her. She listened for a moment but all she could hear was the rain beating harder against the house, the wind forcing the branches of the elm trees to scrape against the red tiled roof. Reassuring herself, she stirred a spoonful of sugar into her coffee before taking it and her sandwich through into the lounge and the unfriendliness of the dying embers in the fireplace.

It took several minutes to rekindle the fire. She sat cross-legged before its warmth on the golden shag pile rug and ate the sandwich. The flames licked higher, spitting every so often as a stray raindrop found its way down the wide chimney. Formless shapes danced around the walls of the unlit room and Alana felt a little uneasy, the only sounds those of the persistent rain outside and the crackling logs within.

She thought of Tom as she gazed into the fire's depths and smiled to herself. In the last few days he had become very important to her. He was special, perhaps even special enough to be permanently part of her life.

Alana had spent many years wandering from one relationship to another, enjoying the sexual experiences each one offered, living each moment for itself alone. She had, she knew, garnered something of a reputation as a man-eater, both at the network and amongst the so-called 'smart' set, but that was too bad. If men went overboard because of her that simply showed them for the weaklings they were.

But Tom *was* different. He was confident, assured of his own abilities; completely in command of his emotions. And sexually he was without equal. Never had she felt so satisfied as she had done these last few days. Without a doubt he was the sort of man a woman dreamed of all her life, but rarely found. If she could help it, she would make damn sure that Alana Kennedy stayed on as his woman!

She jumped as she heard a noise which didn't fit the sounds of the storm and nervously glanced behind as though expecting someone, or something to be in the room. She was alone, and breathed a sigh of relief. She drew her legs up to her chin and sat listening, straining her ears for the slightest sound. And then it came again, for just a moment, soft and slithering, and she felt sure a distorted shape had crossed in front of one of the windows, peering through open curtains into the lounge.

Alana's heart pounded. She could feel the blood rushing in her veins as she rose from the floor and pressed herself against the comforting roughness of the fire surround. Hardly daring to breathe, she inched her way along the wall, past the kitchen door to the stairs. As quietly as she could, she ran up the stairs to Doyle's room and tapped furtively on the door.

'Doyle! Doyle!' she hissed. 'For Christ's sake wake up. There's someone prowling around outside!' She waited a moment longer and then, cursing her somnolent sound-man, she pushed open his door. Even though her catlike eyes had become accustomed to the darkness, she couldn't make out his sleeping form in the bed. A lingering flash of lightning confirmed a sudden fear and she drew her breath in with a gasp at the sight of the empty, undisturbed bed. She was quite alone in the house!

Carefully removing her slippers, she crept back down the stairs, stopping halfway to peer through the wooden railings into the lounge.

Assuring herself that whoever was creeping around had not found his way in, she steeled herself to descend the remaining stairs and then moved quietly across the carpeted floor to the window. Unable to see anything through the inky darkness, she jumped backwards on catching sight of her own reflection in the glass. Alarmed, she suddenly realised she could be seen. A cold chill ran down her spine. The flickering light from the fire provided enough illumination for an observer to watch her every move.

After several minutes' silence Alana had begun to convince herself that she was the victim of an overactive imagination when she heard a noise outside the front door. A milk bottle had been disturbed. She tensed. Both Mott and Doyle had their own keys – there would be no need for either of them to be so stealthy in their approach to the house. The door handle turned slowly, first one way and then the other as an unseen hand tested the lock.

Had she locked the door? Panic-stricken, she searched her memory. Yes. She remembered clearly doing it after they had returned to the cottage. *But Tom had gone out again and so had Doyle!*

Terrified eyes stared with dread towards the door. The handle relaxed and she groaned inwardly as she heard a soft swish-swish as something moved away. The door *was* locked.

Now frozen beside the lounge window she heard again the ominous rustling noise coming nearer. It stopped directly outside and suddenly she saw the malformed shadow cast through the window as another flash of lightning rent the sky. She held her breath, her heart beating against her ribs, until at last she heard the leaden steps retreating. She followed the sound in her mind, knowing the source of her terror was now moving to the rear of the cottage.

Crouching, animal-like, she darted towards the kitchen and fumbled through drawers in a frantic search for the long carving knife. Finally her fingers found the coldness of the sharp blade just as the footsteps rounded the corner of the house and moved purposefully towards the kitchen door.

Alana threw herself to the floor behind the frail-looking stable door and prayed it would be strong enough. The noise came closer and Alana strove to isolate it, place it into a familiar category. But she couldn't.

A noise. Someone was testing the window. She gripped the knife harder, determined she would give a good account of herself if it came to it.

Next the door. She felt a force against the wood and then another as the handle was similarly tried. She leaned back against it with all her strength, trying to add substance and solidity to the wood.

Slow, deliberate footsteps receded, accompanied by the awful noise. The swish-swish-swish reverberated around her head.

Summoning her rapidly diminishing courage, Alana crawled across the kitchen floor into the lounge. She ducked behind the high-backed sofa and peered into the now darkening and unfriendly room, searching the shadows and flickering shapes. Satisfied at last that she was still alone, she crawled across to the far side of the room, her body trembling. Cautiously she raised herself and again peered through the window.

Alana let out a scream as the formless shape rushed at the window towards her from out of the darkness as though it knew this would be the place to which she would come. She saw only the blackness and the strange glint of something reflecting the dying fire. She screamed again.

A hasty rapping at the window caused her to stop and then a familiar, almost comforting voice reached her. 'Miss Kennedy, are you all right?' She ran to the front door and threw it open, glad of the cold rain and wind tearing at her. 'You sonofabitch!' she yelled. 'What the hell do you think you're doing! You scared the shit out of me!'

The miserable-looking Garda officer stepped out of the shadows, his wet cape making the familiar swish-swish as he walked with water dripping onto it from the plastic peak of his police cap, glinting in the hall light. Concerned, Patrick stepped uninvited into the hallway and removed his sodden rain cape.

'I'm sorry, miss, I was just making sure you was all

right, that the place was nice and secure.' Patrick looked cold and unhappy and Alana moved to the drinks trolley and handed him a large tumbler of malt. She suddenly felt foolish, ashamed at having let her imagination run wild.

'And I'm sorry I shouted at you. Come over to the fire, Patrick, and tell me why you're so concerned about our security.'

He moved quickly to the hearth and tossed a few more logs onto the fire, grateful for the whiskey and even more so for the warmth of the flames. After several moments deciding how much to tell the girl, he felt she was experienced enough to face the facts. Patrick had been impressed with the woman's professionalism on the morning Betsy's body had been discovered and he figured if she could stomach the sight of that, then she would be able to stand the latest news. He drained the glass and gratefully accepted a refill from the unhurried Alana. 'There's been three more killings,' he said at last, 'over at Seamus Flynn's place.' He held a hand up to stop the inevitable question. 'No, not Flynn or his missus. An English family camping on his land, down by the little clump of trees. A woman and child raped and murdered. The father mutilated beyond all recognition. I just came by to make sure you were all right in the house, the field just being down the road aways.'

Alana was thunderstruck by the news, but offered the man another drink.

Patrick accepted, glad that this mission wasn't now in vain.

'How did you find them so quickly?' she asked returning the glass.

'Ah well, that was a stroke of luck, so it was. Mrs Flynn herself decided to check on her three scrawny chickens and heard the most terrible screams. She called us and said she thought the father was having a fit or something. One of the constables went along and found them. You didn't see or hear anything, I suppose, did you?'

Alana shook her head. 'No, but they must have been the ones who were looking for accommodation at the pub while we were there.' She told him briefly of the incident and Patrick drained his glass for the third time before reaching for his cape.

As he stepped back out into the rain he turned. 'By the way, Miss Kennedy, I assume you're on your own tonight. Where are the two gentlemen?'

She shrugged. 'Damned if I know, Patrick. But if you see either of them you can tell them they should be ashamed of themselves leaving me alone on a night like this!'

He laughed with surprising gentleness. 'By the size of the knife you were holding when I arrived, I shouldn't have thought you needed either of them around. Well, good night to you. Keep the doors locked.'

She thought of something and called after him: 'Patrick, maybe the butcher didn't kill those people after all, eh?'

He turned again, 'Aye, could be. Good night now.'

'Patrick, what's happening in this village?'

She couldn't see him now, but his words floated through the darkness like a hollow shout from the sea on a foggy night: 'I don't know, miss, but something must be touched with the madness.'

And then he was gone and she hurriedly closed and bolted the door. She pulled the curtains over the windows and returned to the fire, stoking it up so that the flames lit the entire room.

Suddenly she felt afraid. Terribly afraid for herself, for Tom, for Doyle and for the entire village. There was an evil surrounding this place and it was almost as if the small team of journalists had brought something with them which was now tormenting and terrifying this sleepy village.

CHAPTER NINE

The rain drove hard against the window pane. Mott opened his eyes, listening to it for a while as he identified the familiar, comforting sounds drifting from the kitchen below. His body ached and he stretched himself gingerly, ironing the kinks out of his muscular body, before leaving the bed and slipping into his silk dressing gown.

As he shaved in the tiny bathroom, his thoughts wandered over the events of the previous night. He had returned to the cottage after his abortive mission to the village pub to find an unhappy Alana sitting in the darkness. She had told him of the police officer's visit and Tom had agreed with her that it would appear the Craghan murderer was still at large. What he failed to say was that he felt the deaths hadn't been caused by a single person, but by several.

He had recognised Ambrose as being something above an ordinary policeman. This man had the confidence of high office, the sureness of manner which only came with a lifetime of working out of the ordinary milieu of criminology. Mott had seen Ambrose at work, or men exactly like him, in countries throughout the Middle East and Africa. He had recognised the particular touch of the expert interrogator, the sense of total power and ability. No, Ambrose was certainly more than the usual crime squad detective and that meant these crimes being committed here in Roscommon were out of the ordinary as well. Mott had reasoned murders and suicides happened every day of the year, multiple murders less often, but nevertheless they still happened. Therefore it was not so much the killings themselves which had brought Ambrose to the case but the cause behind the deaths.

After Mott had thought over the deaths he had pieced them together in his own mind, isolating the emotive factors. The conclusion he had reached was inescapable. The priest had murdered the two old people – that was one set; the butcher had murdered the spinster – that was a second; the girl Betsy was a third and last evening's triple slaying a fourth – perhaps by the same person.

He felt instinctively that the priest hadn't been slain in the manner the local police believed. It was suicide.

He sluiced his face and towelled it off, noting for the first time the dark circles under his eyes. He combed his raven-black hair and returned to the bedroom to dress.

The 'why' was the most important. Why was it that suddenly a spate of murders, committed by normally sane, intelligent people, had erupted in this village? Alana had mentioned they seemed to have brought bad luck with them. Noble had said much the same sort of thing in Rome, shortly before he'd been killed.

He reached for a cheroot, and walked downstairs. Their filming schedule was right up to date. Only Sunday's shooting remained and after that had been completed he would make plans to leave this place and return directly to the Gulf. He didn't want to face the phoniness of Barbara or his son's awkward attempts to communicate with his father.

Standing at the foot of the stairs he watched Alana moving happily around the kitchen, unaware of his presence. And what of her? There had never been any woman who had really staked a claim on him but if any could it would be Alana. Mott wondered about the sort of life they could have together, toyed with the notion of suggesting she go with him, but then discounted it. Better they parted on Monday as planned. He preferred the solitude of his own company.

As he started to call out to her, a knock at the door made her turn and she beamed a cheery greeting at him. 'I'll get it,' he said, returning the smile.

'Good morning, Mott, I do hope I'm not disturbing you.'

Colonel Ambrose slipped his fine hands from the kid gloves and stepped inside the house. He was tired and the effects of a night's loss of sleep were clearly etched on his face.

'Not at all. You look like you could use some coffee.'

Ambrose nodded. 'Yes indeed, that would be most welcome.'

He followed Mott into the well-equipped kitchen and leaned against the door after a courteous 'hello' to Alana. Mott poured them both a cup and looked quizzically at the officer. 'So what brings you out this early?'

Ambrose unbuttoned his overcoat and extracted a gold cigarette case, lighting up before replying. 'Murder! I'm sure you are aware of the slayings last night. One of the reports stated that neither you, nor your assistant Doyle were at home last night. Perhaps you'd like to tell me where you were?'

Mott drew deeply on his cheroot. 'Do you suspect us of the murders?' he asked softly.

Ambrose shrugged. 'Covering all bases, as you Americans say. The murders happened while you were away from this house. We'd like to know where you were and with whom in order to eliminate you both from our enquiries, standard police procedure, that's all.'

Although he had an alibi, it was one he would have great difficulty in explaining to the officer. His mind raced through the implications of his answer. There was no point in lying. Undoubtedly he had already heard from the publican and was expecting confirmation from Tom. 'I went to the pub to see someone. That's all. I neither saw, nor heard a thing except for a drunk at the back of the bar and, of course, the storm.'

'You were gone quite a while, I understand.'

The police had obviously watched the cottage, waiting to log his return. 'Yes, quite a while.'

'You must have had a lot to talk about with the person you were meeting?'

'He wasn't there.'

Ambrose leaned forward, 'Then why were you so long?'

Mott sighed in exasperation. 'Because I . . . hell, look, would you believe me if I told you I didn't know the name of the guy and I had to wait for the right moment to slip through the back door of the pub and go upstairs?'

'Seems an odd thing to do,' observed Ambrose drily.

'Maybe, but that's the way it was. It's a long story and one which is so crazy it wouldn't make any real sense.'

Ambrose's eyes travelled about the kitchen and settled on a pair of muddied shoes. 'Yours, Mr Mott?'

'Yes.'

'Very muddy! Been walking in the fields, have you?'

'I stepped into a hole behind the pub.'

Ambrose nodded and suddenly lost all interest in them. 'And Mr Doyle, where is he?'

Mott flashed a glance at Alana who shrugged to indicate her own lack of knowledge at the man's whereabouts. 'He's not here. In fact he didn't come home last night.'

Ambrose turned and walked into the lounge, crossing to the high-backed sofa, and slumped into it. His body was tired and drained but his mind was still as crisp as his voice. 'Was he with you at all last evening, with either of you?'

Alana perched on the edge of the settee. 'Yes, earlier. He went upstairs before Tom left. Afterwards, when I thought Patrick was a prowler, I went upstairs to rouse him but he'd gone. His bed hadn't been slept in. I suppose he must have left while I was asleep.'

Ambrose ran a hand over his face thoughtfully. 'Yes, I suppose he must have. Any idea where he went?'

Mott and Alana both shook their heads. 'You don't think he had anything to do with those killings last night, do you?' asked Tom, suddenly realising the significance of the question.

Ambrose looked startled. 'Doyle! Good heavens no! No, I'm sure there is a very good reason for his stopping out last night, but when he does return would you tell him I'd like a word? He can reach me at the local station. I'll be staying until this is over.'

Abruptly, he rose and strode to the door and, without saying goodbye, departed pulling the door shut behind him. Tom and Alana stared at each other briefly and Alana laughed. 'How about that for an exit. Boy, he's really short on manners, isn't he?'

Mott watched the speeding black police car returning the officer to the village. 'Funny thing to say though, wasn't it?'

She joined him at the window and slipped an arm through his, pressing herself against him. 'What was?'

'He said: "I'll be staying until it's over". I should have thought he would have said he would stay until it's cleared up. Just strikes me as a funny way to put it, that's all.'

She thought about it for a moment, but failed to see the distinction and said so. He grinned down at her. 'Forget it. Let's eat.'

As they finished their breakfast, Seamus Flynn arrived to inform them that Doyle's station wagon had been found at the cave entrance. The police had asked him to lead a search party into the winding tunnels as they believed he was probably lost inside.

They drove at full speed to the site, by now alive with teams readying themselves for the search. Police officers checked civilians to ensure that their torches had enough power and that each carried spare batteries; the mobile canteen stood by dispensing hot mugs of tea and soup; ropes were checked for snags or tears and waterproof clothing was dispensed to the first seven-man team, who would make the preliminary inspection of the cave and tunnels.

Standing ominously by was a police ambulance and the nervous figure of a man who Mott recognised as Dr Donavon. If nothing else, the rescue squad was prepared for all contingencies.

For the second time that morning Ambrose greeted them and after apprising the pair of the situation agreed to the American's request that he be included in the search effort. Alana insisted that she also be allowed to join the team. The Colonel was dead set against it, but he finally capitulated, unable to come up with sufficiently forceful reasons as to why she should not be included.

Within fifteen minutes the members of the search party were snaking their way through the initial entrance and passageways, following the lights ahead of them as the main tunnel sloped away into the depths of the earth. They inched their way carefully along for several minutes, stopping to listen for sounds which might give some clue as to Boyle's location. When no sounds came they shouted his name and strained their ears for a response. Still silence. Flynn led the group onward until the next stop where the process was repeated.

In this laborious manner they wound their way ever downwards until eventually they reached the point where Flynn refused to venture further. Sitting down uncomfortably on a protruding rock he looked up at the sergeant in charge.

'Well, sergeant, what do you want to do now? Even I haven't been further than this point. I doubt the man would be so foolish to have gone beyond here, particularly as he knew it was largely unexplored. He must be in one of the tunnels branching off the main one.'

The police officer flashed his torch around. He'd hoped for a quick search resulting in a happy conclusion, enabling him to get out of this dark, eerie place. He turned to Mott: 'You know the man, would he carry on knowing Flynn here hadn't explored the cave further?'

'You'd better ask Miss Kennedy, she knows him better than I do.'

Alana considered the question. She didn't know. Doyle had worked for the network for eighteen months or so, but with her for only the past five. She cast her torch around the ground and then into the tunnel ahead which, if anything, seemed darker, more oppressive than those down which they had already travelled. It was a mystery to her why he should have wanted to come down here alone in the first place. The light from her torch caught something and she moved quickly forward, picking up the object, before turning back to the group excitedly. 'He went on! This is a toggle button from his duffle coat.'

The officer sighed. There was nothing for it, they would have to go on. He instructed one of the younger searchers to retrace his steps back to the surface and inform the rest of the team of their discovery. Flynn drove a flat-headed nail into the hard granite with his mallet, attaching one end of a ball of string to it and paying out a substantial length of the now all-important life-line.

Without the string they ran the risk of suffering the same fate as others who had wandered into the labyrinth.

Three hours later the team entered a large cavern from which ran several more tunnels. Water was dripping from above and the team slumped to the floor exhausted. Sandwiches and hot coffee were passed around. The group munched and drank in silence to the accompaniment of the slow, persistent drip-drip-drip of water from the roof of the cavern.

Alana sat next to Tom and at last voiced what each member of the team was thinking: 'It's hopeless, isn't it, Tom? He could be anywhere, we'll never find him.'

Tom squeezed her arm gently. 'We'll find him. It may take longer, perhaps more men, but we'll find him.'

Flynn threw the dregs of his plastic cup over the ground and spat after it. 'It'll take a bloody army so it will, to search down here. Each of them tunnels could split into seven more and so could each of them. If we find him at all it'll be by sheer good luck, not judgement!'

The sergeant nudged him to keep quiet. 'Well, I think the only thing is to go back up top and report what we've found so far – which is precious little – and get more men down here.'

Alana turned on the man. 'Well I think we should carry on with the search. He could be hurt – maybe close at hand.'

Tom stood and placed a protective arm about her. 'Or he could be miles away. The sergeant's right, we need a much larger search party if these tunnels are to be combed properly, systematically.'

They retraced their way along the string, making sure the nails which had been placed every three hundred yards were still securely entrenched in the walls. The return journey took less than an hour as there was now no need to repeat the slow process of stopping every few minutes. Once on the surface, Ambrose listened intently to their report before putting into motion a full search, utilising the help of the military garrison at Boyle.

The late afternoon hung heavy over the scene and the gathering clouds signalled more bad weather was building over the hills. In the distance, a low roll of thunder sounded like a growl from the earth's depths as it digested the lost remains of the unfortunate Doyle. Alana shivered. She felt threatened by the dark mouth of the cave entrance and couldn't wait to get away.

CHAPTER TEN

Saturday Afternoon, October 30th, Rome

Cardinal Barretta hurried across the busy street before turning onto the Via Appia Antica and walking down the narrow staircase with its worn stone treads. He gave little thought to the millions who had walked this way over the centuries eager to satiate their curiosity; his eyes rigidly ahead in the hot autumn sun he moved with the sense of purpose of a man called to holy mission.

Barretta had received the telephone call at the Cardinal's residency and had changed from his red coat of office to a plain, dark grey, pin-stripe which would blend suitably with the image he wished to project – that of an interested tourist. As the cab sped from the Vatican he wondered why Molinari had insisted they meet at the Catacombs rather than his office. The anxious voice had spoken of a 'matter of great importance to the All Highest'. Had something gone seriously wrong in Craghan?

He joined the small queue of giggling tourists waiting for the afternoon opening of the burial places of the early Christians and checked his watch. It was just on three o'clock. At that moment the gates were swung open and the friars, who acted as guides, moved forward, benevolent smiles of greeting on their faces.

The Cardinal looked around him for the first time, taking in the rough-hewn entranceway with its shaped stones, dug from the soil and shaped by loving hands. He smiled as he overheard a tourist telling a companion how the Christians had hidden in the tombs to avoid the persecution of the Caesars. Obviously information gleaned from watching too many movies. By the end of their tour, the tourist and her friend would learn that the Catacombs were simple burial grounds created by the Christians as a place to honour their dead. The thought that they could be used as hiding places was absurd, particularly as the location of the forty or so catacombs was well known to all citizens of ancient Rome.

The line moved forward as the friars took charge and turned right into the Catacomb of San Callisto, an important series of burial chambers which boasted a great many Popes from the third century. The tourist gabbled on about being in a scene straight out of 'Quo Vadis' and Barretta smiled as he left in the opposite direction, into the Catacomb of San Sebastiano.

A hand touched his arm gently as he did so and he turned to face the cowled figure of a friar. 'The other way, my son, if you please,' said the diminutive figure in soft tones. Barretta smiled gently at the devout monk and raised his right hand slightly, revealing the ring on his third finger. The monk clasped the hand, kissed the ring and murmured apologies as Barretta turned into the tunnel.

A series of weak bulbs cast just sufficient light for him to see and he quickly found his way to the narrow staircase which Molinari had mentioned. He stood at the top and looked down into the depths of the shaft. This was perhaps the oldest of all the burial chambers. Originally a rock quarry, it had been converted into a pagan burial ground before the earliest Christians had taken it over for their own sacred purposes. Now the eerily quiet tombs served as a tourist attraction. He started down the stairs, gripping the metal railing tightly in order to save himself should he slip on the worn steps, half wishing he could still hear the giggling of the young tourists. Chambers of the dead, he thought as he reached the next level, were better left alone as a clandestine meeting place.

It took five minutes for him to reach the bottom level and he stepped nimbly off the last step. He turned and looked back up. The distance seemed greater now than it had done looking down. Even as he started to avert his glance, the lights on the stairway went out, plunging the stairs into a black nightmare of darkness.

Barretta groaned as the lights expired on his level also and he waited, unable to move in the darkness. It wasn't unusual for sudden power cuts to hit the city and the Cardinal knew that tourist facilities invariably had their own generator. There was no need to feel overly concerned. One of the friars would even now be scurrying to the power shack to throw a switch which would send the power rushing through the dead cables.

A weak light flickered in the series of bulbs leading away to his right and then again before holding. It wasn't much but it would be sufficient to avoid stepping into a hole and breaking an ankle. As he moved away from the base of the stairs he glanced upward again. The lights were still out up there. He shrugged. Perhaps they were on a different circuit which hadn't yet been reset by the monks.

The Cardinal moved along the tunnel, peering ahead in search of Molinari. A soft oath forming on his lips at the Monsignor's insistence they meet here. He passed a niche painted with the symbols of a family long since gone and felt a strange sense of familiarity. He had never been here before yet it seemed as though he knew it.

And then the memory flooded back. He had been out of the seminary for no more than six months and had been sent by his bishop to a small mining town in the Catskills. As Father Barretta he had been filled with purpose, resolved to do only the very best for his hard working mining community and had involved himself deeply in the work, caring little that the vast majority were not of the faith he represented. The important thing was to be at one with them, the rest would follow.

Barretta had joined with the Dutch pastor in ensuring that every family was visited at least once a month. They both agreed that it mattered little whether the people they called upon visited their particular place of worship, or indeed, any at all. They would bring His word by virtue of their actions.

The young priest had often thought of that town. Perhaps it was his test. A test to establish his worth and dedication to his calling. He didn't know. He had never spoken of the terrible thing he had done, nor had he ever confessed his sin. How could he and remain within the Church?

He paused as the lights flickered and then, when they held, he moved forward again, recalling the incident.

Carrie Lou Huskins had been, by anyone's standard, an extremely well-developed eighteen year old. She had a lovely face framed by corn blonde hair, long tapering legs and a body which he had heard one of the young men describe as 'heaven, pure heaven'. Deep blue eyes radiated her joy of life and her skin was as fresh as the morning dew on the mountains. She was a beautiful girl and in great demand as her Saturday morning visits to the confessional proved.

For the twenty-four-year-old priest to sit and listen to her pleas for forgiveness after the latest round of debauchery was bad enough, but when the girl decided to set her cap at him it became intolerable. He prayed so very hard for the evil thoughts to go away. He remembered all too well what it was like to lie next to a woman, caress her soft skin and take joy in her.

For a while it had grown easier as he plunged himself into the preparations for the town's annual Labour Day picnic. But she was always around, helping with the balloons or making flags, and she took pleasure in making sly suggestions to him while the young men sniggered in the background. On the day of the picnic she came to the church asking him to hear her confession. He sat in the confessional, separated from her by the curtain, and she recounted how she and a youth had gone to the hills the night before.

He listened to a vivid account of their sexual encounter with a feeling of dulling torpor. He had scarcely believed it was possible to do such things with another human being. And his erection had grown harder and harder as, in his mind, the youth was replaced by himself making love to the beautiful girl.

He didn't know how long Carrie Lou had been fondling him through the parting in the curtain. The realisation had come to him when he had smelt her muskiness and opened his eyes. She stood before him naked, her breasts hanging proudly above his head, her long fingers kneading his groin. The little patch of hair covering her mound was almost in front of his lips and suddenly the feeling was too much and he reached around for her buttocks and drew the body towards him, kissing and biting the slightly pungent hair; his tongue flickered in and out, pushing between her legs searching for the wetness he knew was just beyond.

She moaned, pulling his head deeper into her until the legs parted and his mouth found the clitoris where he ran his tongue, raising her to added heights of ecstasy. She reached frantically for his zip and exposed his upright, rock-hard member and ran light fingers over it for tantalising moments.

Barretta wanted it. All thoughts of his holy orders

were abandoned with the wanton woman. The desire was too much to bear and he pulled her head down and the warm mouth took him in long, slow strokes, that tongue playing over his shaft in the same way it had others. The others she had tormented him with over the months. And it was good!

She straddled him at last in the incredibly small confessional and rode the priest hard, grinding herself down onto him, feeling the tip of his penis penetrating deeper into her. Somewhere in the back of his mind he heard the sounds of the townspeople going to the picnic, laughing on this holiday. And then he climaxed with her in a searing heat of release.

They collapsed against each other and she smothered him with kisses and Barretta felt the terrible shame.

He had left the following week, never to speak of the incident to anyone. He had visited a retreat and gradually the vivid, all too real images of the girl dissolved. After two years he had again taken up his duties and had never fallen again, nor had he ever wished to.

This tunnel reminded him of the mines in that town. He had once gone down the pit to see for himself the conditions his parishioners worked under and had been appalled by them.

He rounded a slight bend and saw Molinari perched incongruously on a rock at the end of the tunnel. He hurried forward, relieved that he had finally located the man.

'I can't say I approve of your choice of meeting-place, Monsignor,' he said irritably.

Molinari smiled. 'I understand your discomfort, but it was necessary. What have you heard from Father Falangi?'

Barretta, a little out of breath, leaned against a rock and replied: 'His plans for preventing Satan's demon from aiding in the entry, through the portal, are almost complete. He is still reasonably strong, strong enough at any rate to complete his task.'

'And the cacodemon?'

Barretta looked thoughtful. 'It's influence is already being felt in the village. Colonel Ambrose tells me there have been several murders, including the local priest, who was murdered after possession of his spirit. But Ambrose called you, surely you know this?'

Molinari nodded and waved an airy hand. 'I need to be able to give as complete a report as possible, even if that means hearing things I am already aware of. Now what of the demon itself? Does Falangi have a plan to stop it before tomorrow night?'

Barretta scuffed at a stone. He had already told Molinari all this and felt extremely annoyed that the Papal Secretary had found it necessary to drag him to this place for a repeat of the report. 'As I told you the other day, Monsignor, Father Falangi intends to manoeuvre it towards a holy place in the hope that he can drive the creature from the host body. Unfortunately, the trap could not be sprung today as Doyle has disappeared. Falangi hopes to attract the demon's interest before tomorrow night.'

Molinari jumped from the stone. 'And, if that doesn't work? What then? What will the good Father do?'

Barretta started to answer as the smell assailed his nostrils. He looked about him as the acrid smell of sulphur filled the tunnel. His eyes watered and he gagged.

'Did you enjoy yourself in the confessional?' The voice was soft and low, spoken with an animal cunning which set the skin alight. Barretta turned back to Molinari, bewildered that the secretary could know his secret.

Molinari appeared to be standing in a yellow haze, his features ebbing and flowing. First solid and then like liquid as the sulphur fumes swirled around his legs, enveloping his body. And Molinari stared at him with a lascivious grin, eyes shining with an eerie intensity.

Barretta could not turn his gaze from the glinting eyes and with total terror he watched them change shape into slanted cat's eyes. Then the entire shape dissolved as the figure of Molinari was replaced with that of Satan's demon. It stood before him completely naked. Huge breasts hanging from its chest with a massive, erect organ held in one hand. The face was grotesque and again it shifted until it became the face of the girl in the Catskills.

Cloven feet shuffled forward and the hideous creature breathed its foul breath over the Cardinal. 'Suck my cock the way she sucked yours,' it commanded in a flat, toneless voice.

Barretta felt the foul thing forced between his teeth. Hard as stone, large blue veins running down the impossible length. He gagged as it was pushed further down his throat and frantically he reached into his pocket for the phial of holy water.

The incubus smashed the Cardinal's hand against the wall. 'No good this time, priest,' it stated as the precious liquid was wasted, 'your god has given you up. You're ours now. For all eternity you're ours!'

The demon withdrew from Barretta's mouth and he vomited onto the floor, bending double in great, heaving gasps. He felt his suit being ripped from his body as the demonic spirit stripped him and he cared little as the demon mounted him, thrusting his enormous phallus deep into Barretta's anus.

The sound of Barretta's scream, as vital organs were penetrated, reverberated around the corridors of the dead, then the lights came on again throughout the Catacomb of San Sebastiano.

Doyle shifted his weight with care and winced as the stabbing pain raced up his shattered leg. A wave of nausea swept over him. Even in this cold tomb of a place, he was sweating profusely, having to stop his ponderous crawl to wipe his eyes of the stinging droplets.

He ran a cautious hand back down the right leg and gently fingered the protruding bone with its jagged end. A thought flashed through his mind that if he didn't get help soon he was in danger of losing the leg. He grimaced at that. Hell, if he didn't get help he would be losing more than his leg! He ran a finger over the Rolex on his left wrist and cursed as he touched broken glass. It didn't really matter anyway, he had lost the torch and without it he was unable to read the dial.

The soundman gritted his teeth and, taking a deep breath, he placed his hands on the cold, wet floor and pushed. He experienced an excruciating pain as his body moved backwards until gratefully, he felt the smooth tunnel walls against his back and he relaxed. He lay there without moving, gulping mouthfuls of air into tortured lungs, willing the pain to subside and cursing his own stupidity. As the pain ebbed he thought back over the events which had brought him here.

It had all really begun two years ago when, because of his prowess as a marksman, he had been detailed to join the Pope's security team during the Pontiff's state visit to Ireland. At first, it had been an experience to rival all others. Even the hard-bitten security force had been moved by this Catholic leader's devotion and by the genuine affection shown to him by the millions who came to see him during his visit. It was as though the Pope had brought with him a peace and tranquillity rarely seen in this troubled land.

And then, suddenly, it all seemed to fall apart. Not from terrorists, although there were plenty of threats against the man's life, but from an intangible source Doyle hadn't fully understood.

After the Pope had visited the town of Knock with its holy shrine, Doyle and his partner had been ordered to establish a listening post at Dragha Abbey to ensure the area was 'clean'. They had spent a cold, depressing night wondering why this place rated full treatment when it wasn't scheduled on the Pontiff's itinerary. Shortly before dawn their radio had squawked into life, informing them that the Pope was entering the grounds on an unscheduled, private visit.

Fifteen minutes later they logged the car travelling back along the gravel driveway at speed, unusual for O'Casey. Doyle had watched the vehicle swerve and plunge off the road into a small clump of trees. What followed was blurred in his mind for many months after. He recalled drawing his pistol and, with his partner, racing over to the saloon car where, for the first time, he stood beside the holy man and his aide.

His partner had drawn away from the car visibly shaken and had left the service after the experience, unable to come to terms with the strange forces at work. Doyle threw almost a casual glance at the twisted head of the dead driver. After the Pope had been transferred to another vehicle, the car had exploded and Doyle had stood with Colonel Ambrose watching the flames as they licked higher and higher. Early the next day a report had come through that lightning had seared across the sky in one long, brilliant bolt and had struck at the heart of the beautiful Abbey; the monks burnt to death as they slept.

But for Doyle, it had not ended. Many sleepless nights and vivid nightmares had followed. Eventually, he had sought the help of the department's psychiatrist. When he was finally released from the hospital, Ambrose had summoned him to O'Connell Street. Unexpectedly, no mention was made of his treatment. He was told he had been scheduled to take a course in sound recording preparatory to his joining RTE. He assumed they had discovered another nest of IRA sympathisers and was surprised after his course to learn that he was to become a 'sleeper'. Ambrose informed him at a second interview that, in a little over a year, a man would arrive and Doyle would be assigned to watch him. It would be made easier by RTE, who would follow the security service's request by assigning him to this man.

Although it was odd, Doyle knew better than to query the Colonel. Security worked in strange ways and Doyle settled down to await his new mission. Five months before Mott arrived, Doyle had been teamed up with the beautiful camera woman and then right on schedule, Mott had walked into his life and Alana out.

Doyle tried to draw the broken leg towards him and abandoned the effort as the pain throbbed mercilessly through the limb. He cursed Mott, wishing he hadn't overheard the American talking to Alana.

The Irishman had gone to his own room with the intention of getting right into bed but had decided against it when he had heard the excited voices of the lovers in the room next to his. When it became apparent that Mott was about to leave the house again, Doyle had slipped downstairs and quietly let himself out to sit waiting in the station wagon.

He had watched Tom leave, walking with hurried steps towards the village, and waited until he was almost around the bend in the road before starting the car and moving after his quarry. As he did so, the rain started. Not the normal light drizzle so familiar in Ireland, but a sudden, torrential downpour that obscured the way ahead.

As he drove into the village he could see no sign of Mott. If Mott was meeting someone, the Colonel would want to know who and he wouldn't accept Doyle's excuse that a violent rainstorm had caused the experienced officer to lose him. He left the car and ran to the smoke-encrusted, yellowing windows of the pub and scanned the single bar. Mott was not there.

Standing in the downpour, he looked first one way and then the other along Craghan's single main road. He must have walked through the village towards the crossroads. He ran back to the car and started driving, carefully scrutinising the few doorways along his route in case Mott was taking shelter.

Doyle breathed a sigh of relief as he spotted the figure walking briskly up the side of the hill, head bowed against driving wind and rain, towards the cave entrance. Turning off the vehicle's headlights he drove on, trusting the sidelights would illuminate the narrow roadway sufficiently for him to avoid driving over the edge. Five hundred yards from the cave's mouth he turned these off and coasted to a standstill in complete darkness.

He held his right arm up to protect his face from the rain which seemed to intensify once he left the car. The hillside was completely barren and as far as he could determine he was the only person around. Mott must have entered the cave and if so, Ambrose would want to know why.

Doyle judged he had been in pursuit for almost an hour as he entered a large cavernous area well beyond the perimeter that Flynn had explored. A steady drip of water sounded first from one section and then another and Doyle snapped the torch on to get a better look at the place.

Huge stalactites hung from the ceiling, reaching with glistening tips for their counterparts thrusting up from the cavern's floor. The walls winked at him as the torchlight passed across veins of green, or touched briefly on crystalline shapes embedded in golden sandstone. On both the walls and floor grew a profusion of moss and clumps of lichen, tinged grey and yellow, and he spotted the skeletal remains of a small creature which had evidently wandered inside the labyrinth and died of starvation.

He moved forward and his leg bumped into a stalagmite, breaking it off, to send it careering across the floor in a noisy, reverberating sound which would disturb the dead, let alone someone like Tom Mott! He snapped off the light and waited a few moments to see if the noise would attract attention. In the stillness he thought he detected a strange sulphuric odour but suddenly it was gone. He felt safe, so he crept towards one of the seven branch tunnels where he had discerned the soft glow of a receding torch.

Doyle reached the end of the tunnel. A solid granite wall faced him and as far as he could be sure in the gloom, he hadn't missed an exit. He retraced his steps back to the cavern, but this time he swung the torch light over the ceiling and down, along both sides of the tunnel. If the figure he'd been following hadn't evaporated into thin air, there must be a hole into which he had disappeared. He was almost at the end of the tunnel when he discovered a narrow fissure lying just above floor level in the left hand wall.

He slipped inside and began a slow, tortuously claustrophobic crawl along its length, all the while wondering how the large frame of Tom Mott had ever been able to navigate so small an aperture.

And then he fell! Without the benefit of the torch to warn him, the floor of the passageway suddenly vanished beneath him and sent him hurtling to the ground fifteen feet below. His leg snapped like a matchstick and his head smashed in piercing agony against an outcrop.

When he awoke some time later, he found his leg doubled up under him, his torch lost in the darkness. A sticky, congealing patch covered the left side of his face and Doyle remembered bitterly the stories Flynn had told of the other people who had been lost inside the system of tunnels.

Many hours had passed. Doyle thought it about six, but it was nearer twenty. He assured himself that help would come soon, very soon. His eyelids felt heavy and he fought hard against the blackout which threatened to overwhelm him. He was slipping slowly into unconsciousness, unaware that two search parties had already been and gone, and with them all hope of ever locating him.

CHAPTER ELEVEN

Sunday, October 31st

Sunday morning in Craghan, like Sunday mornings everywhere, is a time for relaxation; a time when the alarm clock is not set, when the body clock alone is used to waken slumbering residents to the familiar quiet of the seventh day. There is no mailman to slam gates in the early hours; no barking dogs; no garbagemen to drop lids carelessly to the ground, in spiteful reminder that they have been working these many hours past. There is only the chirping of the birds and the sound of the odd car making good time on the traffic-free road.

Eventually the sleeping populace is disturbed, in a sort of dreamlike way, by the sound of the whistling paper boy as he pops the fat *Sunday Times* through the letter box or teases the neighbour's dog with the *Sunday Mirror*. And even that noise has its place among the stillness and peace of the day of rest.

In Craghan this Sunday morning, sleeping males were prodded into wakefulness by wives or lovers as the first sounds of St Bernadette's church bell rang across the village. It was time to hurry if they were not to be late for Mass. The agnostic, the protestant and the bachelor turned over at the sound and slept for another hour. For them, the bell to listen for was the one which announced twelve o'clock and the opening of the King's Arms.

Following the death of Father Michael, a notice had been pinned to the church notice board announcing to the faithful that a temporary priest would say Mass on

Sundays until a permanent replacement arrived to take over the duties. As little floral hats were pinned to straggly hair, the Catholic women wondered what this substitute would be like and whether he would make any reference to the untimely death of dear Father Michael. By the time they flocked through the doors of the church at eleven forty-five, the women could hardly contain their curiosity.

John MacMahon came fully awake and stared up at the brown stain on the ceiling. Every day for the past two years he had woken, looked at the stain and resolved to do something about the loose tile on the roof. This morning as he looked at the spreading mark he made no such promise to himself. Instead he lay there thinking about the nightmare he had experienced during the night. Perhaps nightmare wasn't quite the right word for it. Dream was better. It hadn't frightened him, in fact, it made him feel – different, wanted, warm. That was it, the dream had made him feel a *part* of something.

MacMahon didn't like this village. Hadn't liked it since the day he had come here to marry Elizabeth. That had been a mistake! There he was, happy as a pig in the proverbial, up in the hills, tending the flocks of sheep which the valley farmers entrusted into his care, when along came the slip of a thing – all cow-eyed and panting.

The shepherd had helped her on her way to womanhood and been happy enough to service the girl at weekends. And then she had come to him with her troubles, insisting he marry her. Reluctantly, MacMahon had left his beloved solitude and moved down into the village. It was then he heard the sniggers from the other men in the pub and at market. Elizabeth was the bloody village bicycle – every man around had ridden her!

Still, he had stuck by her and made the best of things. He was a good worker and his services as an unofficial veterinary supplemented the pay he received working on the Crogan's farm. The trouble was he could never forget the sniggers nor the creeping doubt that while Elizabeth was the mother of their eldest child he may not be the father! There was no doubt about the other two, they were his all right. He made good and sure Elizabeth had no time to get up to her old tricks.

And then there were the villagers themselves. They didn't like him. He could tell by the way they avoided him. Oh, there was nothing tangible of course, just the odd little thing like not including him in a round when he'd been standing at the bar for half an hour and talking as nice as could be with them. Things like that made him understand that he was useful on occasion to all of them, but they didn't expect him to get too friendly. The line was drawn.

She slammed a door somewhere in the house and he winced. Why did she insist on doing that? The bloody woman still hadn't learned to use the friggin' door handles after all this time, after all his shouting at her. The door slammed again, shaking the upstairs and he grew angrier as he lay on his back. She would be rushing around getting ready for church, wiping the kids' faces, making sure the new baby had a dry nappy on. Soon she would pound her flat-footed way up the bare stairs and stand in the doorway looking at him with the insolence rising in her high-pitched voice: 'Are you not coming to the church again?' she would say.

'I'm not', would be the reply and she would sneer at him as he lay there before turning on her heels and stomping back down the stairs to leave the house with a final slam of the front door, shattering any thoughts of another half-hour before the pub. How could a man settle after all that racket?

The bottom step creaked and he knew she was about

to commence the routine. He grinned to himself and slipped from the bed and ducked into the wardrobe. This Sunday he would change the script and give her a fright before she could storm out of the house.

The bedroom door opened and his wife stepped into the room, her back to the old walnut wardrobe, and he heard her say: 'Are you not com . . .', before she broke off in surprise at the sight of the empty bed. MacMahon stepped from the wardrobe, grabbed his wife by the shoulders and spun her around.

Elizabeth looked up at him in surprise and the laugh that formed in her throat died away as she saw the strange light flash from his eyes. She couldn't speak and didn't understand what was happening until she felt the strong hands grip her throat and start to squeeze the life from her body. She brought her knee up hard and fast into his groin, the way he had taught her. He only grinned wider at her efforts to rupture him and he applied greater pressure, savouring the sight of the life being extinguished from her overweight body.

Just before she slipped into unconsciousness he released the powerful grip, allowing her to breathe again. He helped her over to the bed and listened as she gasped painfully for air. Then he reached across, gripped her head and snapped her neck.

MacMahon dressed carefully in his Sunday suit and walked downstairs. His two eldest children were teasing the baby and he greeted them cheerily, telling them their mother would be with them in a moment. He then moved into the dirty kitchen and turned off the dripping cold water tap before locating the scythe he had brought home from the farm to sharpen only the day before. The shepherd ran a thumb over the edge of the blade. Perfect! If nothing else, coming to the village had taught him the correct way to hone a blade.

He took the tool into the small living room and, with one sweep of the instrument, decapitated the two boys. As their small bodies crumpled to the floor, blood spurted from severed arteries and the hot sticky liquid splattered over the baby, startling it into screaming action.

MacMahon crossed to the pram and, oblivious of the blood covering his best suit, picked the baby up, and, summoning all his might, dashed its fragile body against the wall dislodging the three plaster geese in mid flight.

With a feeling of satisfaction, he left the house and walked towards the pub for his Sunday drink, not caring that his feet squelched from the blood in his shoes and oblivious of the sight he presented.

The dream had been right. All his troubles were over now *they* were gone. Now he belonged.

Patrick replaced the field telephone and turned to face the man he knew only as Colonel Ambrose. He disliked this man intensely. He hated the assured manner with which he had arrived and taken over the search for Doyle; disliked the way senior Garda officers kowtowed to him, like servile waiters afraid of causing offence; was irritated by the man's gloves and the way he worked them so carefully on and off fingers that were more like a woman's; and most of all he was afraid of the power the Colonel obviously had. But perhaps what niggled him most was the way in which Ambrose had moved in, taken over, his own police station! Patrick prided himself on his police post and always made sure that everything was kept in just the right place. The files were neat and orderly, the waste basket emptied both morning and afternoon. Neat and orderly! But Ambrose treated the place like a pit. Papers everywhere, pipe tobacco scattered carelessly, telephone cords twisted. It was just all a bit too much.

Had it been one of his own superiors it would have been a different matter but the Colonel had nothing to do with him. Enough was enough.

Ambrose looked expectantly at the Garda officer. 'Well?'

'The army say they have just about combed the entire system, sir, nothing found except a few old bones. The Captain is sure Doyle can't be in the system at all.'

Ambrose thought over the implications of the report. 'Anything else?'

'Yes sir. He says unless you object or instruct otherwise they will make one final check of the last tunnel and then switch the search to the moorland. He's already asked for helicopter reconnaissance of the ground.'

Ambrose nodded. They wouldn't find Doyle, not alive anyway, he was now certain of that. Doyle had gone into the cave, but why remained a mystery. Doyle could always be relied upon to obey an order. His orders had been to watch Mott, not to go off alone into the damned cave without proper equipment or back-up.

Patrick coughed and Ambrose looked up at the man, eyebrows raised. He had obviously spoken and the Colonel had been so deeply into his own thoughts that he hadn't heard. 'I'm sorry, what did you say?'

'I said a box arrived for you during the night. I put it into the cell for safekeeping.'

'Strange, I wasn't expecting anything.' Patrick shrugged indifferently and asked if he wanted to see it anyway. Intrigued, Colonel Ambrose followed the policeman to the single cell at the back of the small station, behind the storeroom. The cell was rarely used for anything more serious than a Saturday night drunk and even then it was more for his own good than to satisfy any law.

Patrick stopped at the solid-looking door with its sheet metal covering and reached for the large key which was kept securely out of reach of probing fingers. He unlocked the door and ushered Ambrose inside.

A lifetime spent dealing with the worst elements of criminal society had sharpened the Colonel's instincts and he moved to his left in a reflex action even as he felt the air behind him disturbed by a fast-moving object. He whirled about, driving a fist with a speed and hardness that belied his frame, into Patrick's face. The truncheon flew from the man's hand as his body staggered against the opposite wall.

Before Ambrose could slip from the narrow cell, Patrick had launched himself at him again with a deep snarl which sounded more animal than human. Spittle ran uncontrollably from his mouth in great, white rivulets and the Colonel became aware of the smell. He had experienced it only once before, at Craghan Abbey, when he had peered inside the car containing the dead security agent. He spent too long thinking about the odour rather than defending himself and Patrick seized him around the neck in a head-lock with one inhumanly strong arm. Ambrose raised his hands to try to break the stranglehold; then stubby fingers gouged into his eyes and he felt the tears running down his cheeks. *The man was trying to tear his eyes out!* If he didn't act now, he would be blinded. With a supreme effort he turned his assailant around, released his own grip on Patrick's arm and, with the first two fingers of his left hand, jabbed hard and viciously into his eyes. At the same time, he brought his right hand up in a cutting slash against Patrick's windpipe.

The policeman screeched in pain and fell away from Ambrose, clutching at his throat. One eye hung loose from its socket and from the other a thin trickle of clear fluid coursed a lazy path towards the officer's open mouth.

Ambrose staggered to the door, himself half-blinded. Once in the corridor he slammed the door into place, trembling fingers turning the key before Patrick could recover his wits.

Patrick lunged at the cell door, cursed Ambrose and spat a large wad of phlegm at the man. The stench in the confined space was overpowering and Ambrose felt the bile rising in his stomach. Suddenly, Patrick began to laugh. Low and soft at first and then rising to a crescendo of evil cackling as, with a last assault, the demon possessing the unfortunate Patrick's body took hold of the loose eye and, ripping it from the retaining membrane, hurled the iris at the Colonel.

Ambrose vomited over the floor and shuffled back to the office, the laughter ringing in his ears. For several long moments he made an attempt to regain his composure and then, swiftly, dialled a Dublin number. As he stood leaning against the desk, a kid leather glove held to his own damaged eye, he watched a man across the street walking with determination towards the pub.

He spoke rapidly to the duty officer, ordering him to seal off the village again. He replaced the telephone and watched the blood-soaked John MacMahon enter the pub for his Sunday drink.

As Colonel Ambrose talked with his Dublin office, Seamus Flynn stood in the doorway of his daughter's bedroom and gazed lovingly at the sleeping form. That such an ugly old man as he could have sired such an attractive gentle girl was a constant source of bewilderment and joy.

He had been filled with pride twenty years ago when the swelling in his wife's body had produced the baby girl and over the years the lack of money in their life had been replaced by the bounty of her existence, bringing into a hard life a great deal of happiness and pleasure.

It was true that they had been somewhat disappointed when she had talked to them of her intention to join the convent. His wife and he had often dreamt of their girl marrying a handsome young man and giving them beautiful grandchildren. His wife had imagined that the man would be rich and they would visit them on a Sunday afternoon to take tea in a sumptuous drawing room overlooking immaculately tended grounds where the nanny would be walking the children.

But a nun in the family was all right too. There had been what . . . two priests ordained from the village? – that was it, two. But no nuns. Their own little Christine would be the first. The girl had brought none of the troubles that one might expect. No boyfriends hanging around trying to get to know her too well. She had always wanted to give herself only to Christ and she remained pure of thought and body waiting for the moment when she would enter the convent. It was to be a long education which would result in the habit of the Carmelites being placed over her beautiful rich red hair.

A sudden thought struck Seamus. What about young Ryan? He seemed to hold a special place in her affections. Had he managed to deflower his precious child? Had he taken away the offering that was Christ's alone? Seamus looked at the girl, at her chest gently rising as she breathed. There was only one way to be sure.

Seamus unbuckled the wide leather belt around his waist and stepped from the only decent pair of trousers he possessed. He threw his shirt and tie onto her dressing-table and then stepped out of his underwear before walking around to the side of the bed nearest the window. Gently he pulled back the duvet and slid into the warmth without disturbing the sleeping woman.

He lay there for a moment before reaching for her soft breasts and fondling them. Christine stirred in her disturbed slumber as unfamiliar sensations rippled through her body. Seamus ran his hand gently between her legs and felt the stiffness of her patch of short hair, and probed deeper.

Christine opened her eyes with a bewildered expression as her father's fingers found their target. She turned uncomprehendingly towards him and he moved, smothering her gentle mouth with rough, harsh kisses.

When the girl struggled he pressed harder, excited by the wriggling of the lithe body beneath him. Her night dress was ripped and she moaned with horror and disgust at what was happening.

He prised her legs apart and noted with satisfaction his own erection. He had known he would be able to do it, known he could get it up again. It had just been waiting for the right moment, the right opportunity!

As he forced himself into his daughter he gripped both large breasts with calloused hands and held on as she bucked and wriggled. The movements only served to aid the penetration and then he felt the hymen rupture. So she was a virgin! That's nice!

He rose and fell on his daughter and she screamed in pain and anguish.

Seamus turned as his wife entered the room and grinned at her through blackened teeth, the light shining brightly from his eyes. 'After I've finished with this whore,' he snarled, 'I'll take you!'

On the other side of the village, in the small house set aside for the parish priest, the clergyman rose and walked stiffly into the bathroom where he showered and shaved, ensuring every last vestige of hair be removed. Then he returned to the bedroom and dressed with more care than usual. Without a backward glance at the room, he moved to the kitchen and poured himself a strong cup of coffee from the automatic percolator. Carrying the cup he walked to the front room and stared, without really seeing, into the street and along Craghan's main road.

He saw the paper boy cycling lazily along, his bag straining with the day's papers, and watched as Colonel Ambrose arrived at the small police station. The priest looked up at the sky and witnessed the change. Swirling off-white clouds merged with large billowing black ones and the whole perspective tinged with a sickening yellow that bespoke of the terrible evil which was falling over the small community.

The priest sighed unhappily, replaced the coffee cup in the wall rack and left the house, walking across the small, well-kept garden to the church to prepare for Mass.

CHAPTER TWELVE

Tom Mott burrowed deeper under the warm covers, fondling Alana and vaguely wishing the alarm clock hadn't clamoured its reminder that they must rise and resume the search for Doyle. Today was Sunday and Doyle was obviously still missing. Would RTE send another soundman to replace him? He thought so, they would be as concerned as he to finish the last stages of the documentary. Alana would have to work closely with the replacement to ensure the sound level was correct, recorded at the same level as the previous tapes. New York wouldn't appreciate too many highs and lows on the broadcast tape.

Alana stirred sleepily and Mott wondered what sort of a night Doyle himself had had. They had both stayed with the search party until late evening, giving up to get some much needed rest only when Mott had begun to doubt that Alana would be able to handle her side of the following day's shooting. If nothing else, he would ensure the film was not endangered.

She opened her eyes and rolled into his arms, content after a full night's sleep. Mott had been concerned that she might lie awake, worrying over her lost colleague, but fortunately within a matter of seconds of climbing into bed, sleep had overtaken her.

'Do you think they've found him yet?' she asked, barely awake.

'Doubt it. Somebody would have been along to let us

know by now. But don't worry, I'm sure they'll find him before long.'

She sat upright, leaning on one arm, and looked at him. 'I think he must be hurt. The search party could have passed him by a dozen times and missed him, particularly if he was unconscious and unable to call out.'

He reached for her, feeling the desire rising in his loins and she pulled away, slightly irritated that he didn't show more concern for Doyle. He reached for her again and she threw back the covers and stepped out of bed. He admired her nakedness, his eyes travelling over her smooth skin, taking in her firm jutting breasts and flat stomach. He grinned and indicated she should return to the bed.

She shook her head: 'Not now, Tom, I'm going to get dressed and up to the cave and see if there is any news. I suggest you get on the phone and call Dublin. Ask for Michael Cameron – he's the assignment editor on the weekends – and tell him we need a new man for the day. He'll scream blue murder over the cost but you'll pull more rank than I can. Now I'm for the shower.'

Tom listened to the sound of the water and after a moment he too got out of the bed and put on a pair of faded blue jeans and denim shirt before going downstairs to start coffee. He thought briefly about lighting the fire but discounted it in favour of setting it for when they returned that evening. It was going to be a long day and he knew he wouldn't feel like making it when they returned from filming.

Suddenly he caught sight of a piece of paper stuck through the letter box. He walked over quickly, it was probably a message from the police about Doyle. As he started to open it, Alana walked up behind him, smelling fresh from her shower. 'What is it?' she asked peering over his shoulder.

'A note, I guess,' he replied as he drew the double-folded paper from its envelope. He saw the printed words 'St Bernadette's Church' in bold type at the head of the paper and below them the name of the village. The message itself was written in shaky handwriting.

Would you please come to the church at about one o'clock this afternoon.
It is most important and in part concerns your colleague Doyle. Thank you!

Mott turned the page over and then back again. There was no signature on the paper. 'I wonder who it's from,' he muttered.

'Someone who wants to see us at one o'clock,' she replied light-heartedly. 'Now if you want to look good on camera you'd better go take a shower. I'm good, but even I couldn't hide that dirty hair with the strands of cobwebs running through it.'

Tom ran his hands through his hair and did indeed pull away a handful of filmy spider's web evidently harvested the previous day on their search through the cave. He made a face and walked towards the stairs, checking his watch as he went. It was just after twelve, not much time if he were to meet the person who fed the note through the letter box during the night.

'Are you going to come with me?' he shouted down the stairs.

'No, Doyle is more important than meeting some crank who probably has a pet theory on where he is. But I will call Dublin if you like, but I don't guarantee I'll have any success with Cameron. He's a mean bastard.'

He opened the shower door calling out before he stepped inside the cubicle: 'Promise him you'll sleep with him – that'll do it.'

Her retort was lost as he turned the taps on, gratefully subjecting his body to the invigorating needles of water. At last he felt clean and stepped from the shower to find Alana sitting on the side of the bath, a strange expression on her face.

'Are you all right?'

She looked at him, her face white. 'I feel bloody terrible. Dizzy and nauseous. It just came over me. Christ, I hope I didn't catch a cold down that damn tunnel!'

He poured a glass of water for her and sat next to her. After a while she claimed she felt much better. Tom was still concerned and she tried to reassure him. 'I'm fine, truly. Probably just the whole experience of yesterday catching up with me. Look, I've got to get into the village to call Cameron and then I'll see you later. Okay?'

He nodded. 'Okay, but you take care and no going into the cave on a search. I need you fresh and ready to do your job. Understand?'

Alana studied him for a moment, a cruel remark playing on her lips. He was so totally unconcerned about Doyle, caring only for his film and making sure they didn't lose the day's production. She fumed and then stalked from the room without further word.

As she raced her sports car towards the village, Mott stood at the window watching her, impassively. Then he turned and dressed again in the same outfit and moved about the bedroom collecting his things, preparing them in the same way he always did.

That done, he left the house and climbed into Doyle's station wagon which he had brought down from the cave the previous night, and drove slowly in the direction of the village.

He pushed open the impressive wooden doors to the

church and stepped inside, pausing for a moment as his eyes adjusted to the gloomy interior. He could smell incense burning, an oppressive smell which had always sickened him to the point of giddiness. He walked to the aisle and moved towards the altar, his footsteps ringing hollow in the church as his shoes hit the polished granite slabs.

It was dark inside the church, with scant relief coming from a large stained glass window set high in the eaves above the marble altar and from three solitary candles burning under the statue of the Virgin and Child. To his right stood the black confessional box topped with an ornate grill far too splendid for a country church. Around the walls hung twelve plaster plaques denoting the various stages of Christ's life, known to the faithful who worshipped here as Stations of the Cross. Hymn books lay scattered on benches, evidence that the congregation had not long since been gone.

As he neared the altar rail, he turned around to look down the church. It was now past one o'clock and there was no sign of anyone. Glancing up his eyes passed over the blackened beams and the choir loft.

The American again checked his watch and on looking around him spotted for the first time, a small arched door set into the thick walls, just to the left of the altar. It would lead to the Sacristy. He moved quickly around the altar rails towards the door and tested the handle. It moved easily and he stepped through into the pitch-black room.

Running a hand over the cold stone wall he searched for the light switch and cursed softly when he couldn't locate one. At the far end of the chamber he thought he could discern the shape of yet another door and he moved towards it.

Behind him the door which led back to the church

slammed shut with a finality that made him jump but he continued to inch his way forward, arms outstretched to avoid any obstacles.

He had gone only a few yards when he felt something grasp his legs. In an instant he had been propelled onto the hard floor, his head smashing painfully against a metal locker. He kicked out wildly and felt the thing lift into the air with the movement, swirl and then fall on his head almost smothering him.

Forcefully, Mott pulled it from his face and rolled in the direction of the far door. Reaching it, he stood upright and groped around the hard stone for the light switch. His fingers found it and the room was suddenly flooded with light.

Crumpled on the floor his assailant lay immobile. It was a discarded choirboy's surplice. He walked over, picked it up and rehung it behind the door on a hook, berating the recalcitrant, unknown boy as he did so.

Mott checked the door, found it was locked and returned to the other door which would lead him back into the church. Whoever had sent him the note wasn't coming and he resolved to get to the cave to ensure that their preparations were still secure. In particular, he wanted to talk with Flynn to ensure the man wasn't thinking of calling off the rituals. That was the most important of all.

He slipped quietly back into the church and, on moving towards the aisle, spotted a man in the third pew with head bowed, seemingly deep in prayer. It was Ambrose! He might have known it would be him. He walked purposefully towards the man when a figure stepped from behind the pulpit and touched him lightly on the arm.

Mott swung around and stared with disbelief into the weary eyes of Father Falangi. 'You!' he exclaimed.

'Hello Mr Mott, how are you?' replied the priest in his soft voice, 'it was good of you to come.'

Mott was aware that Ambrose had left his seat and now stood just behind his left shoulder. He glanced back at the Colonel and then returned his level gaze to the priest. 'What's going on Father?' he asked with a soft threatening tone in his voice.

'You have every reason to be angry with me, my son, and I promise you that I shall reveal everything to you in good time, but for the moment I do ask you to be patient.' He looked past Mott and addressed himself to Ambrose. 'Thank you, Colonel, I shall handle it from here. You know what you must do?'

The Colonel nodded and started to walk away from them. Then, almost as a second thought, he turned back and placed a hand on the old priest's shoulder and squeezed gently. The priest patted the hand, 'thank you, my son, now go.' Ambrose walked quickly down the aisle and out of the church leaving Falangi and the American alone.

'Miss Kennedy is not with you?'

'No, she's busy,' Mott replied, slightly irritated.

Falangi indicated they should sit in the front pew, well worn from generations of worshippers. Mott sat, waiting for Falangi to provide explanations for the events in Rome and for his unexpected presence in this small Irish village. Falangi gathered his thoughts for a moment and then began to speak in hushed tones:

'What I am about to tell you is something you will not believe. Indeed, until 1956 I don't suppose I would have believed it myself. Since that time, however, I have learned many things and have been subjected to the worst abominations it is possible to imagine. My story concerns the fight between good and evil. Not the form we see about us every day but the purest form of good and, if it's not a contradiction in terms, the purest form of evil.'

He breathed laboriously and looked towards the stained-glass scene of the crucifixion above the altar as though summoning strength from it before continuing. 'The Devil *does* exist, Mr Mott. His form is quite hideous, reflecting the sins and crimes of this sad world, which he wants for his own dominion – I know because I have seen him. Not once but many, many times.'

The old priest smiled at the undisguised cynicism in Mott's face. 'I dare say you think me mad. Well I assure you that, while I have often feared for my sanity, at the moment I am quite sane. How old would you say I am?'

Mott studied the gaunt face. Two weeks ago he would have thought late sixty, but now the man looked closer to eighty. He ventured sixty. The priest clasped his arm earnestly.

'In 1956 when this all began for me, I was a young prelate, working in your own United States. I was twenty-three years old then.'

Mott mentally calculated. 'That's not possible,' he exclaimed, 'that would mean you're only . . .'

'Forty-eight years of age. Yes, I know. The body you see before you is one which has endured the most intense suffering at the hands of Satan and his foul hordes. Every day and night for the last two years I have been tormented both mentally and physically in an attempt to sway me from the task given me twenty-five years ago. A task which involves you, even though you are an unknowing and unwilling participant.'

A tingling sensation ran through Mott at the old man's words. He had thought Falangi was mad and now began to wonder if he was dangerous too. 'And how do you come to that conclusion?' he asked tersely.

'I cannot explain everything just at the moment, but

suffice it to say I arranged for the theft of the document in your care in the hope that you would track down my whereabouts. I need you here at this time in order that all the elements be in position if I am to be able to prevent Satan from crossing over.'

Mott snorted with derision. 'Oh, come on, Father, this is ridiculous. Are you telling me that you really believe the old legends about a portal being located somewhere in the cave?'

Falangi nodded carefully. 'I know there is. You see, I have spent the last twenty-five years locating the door through which he will enter the surface world, at the end of his thousand years of imprisonment. You remember I told you to look up a chapter in Revelations?'

'Yes.'

'Did you?'

'Yes.'

'And?'

Mott laughed. 'You don't really expect me to give credence to that, surely, Father?'

Falangi closed his eyes, remembering the passage. 'And cast him into the bottomless pit and shut him up and set a seal upon him that he should deceive the nations no more till the thousand years should be fulfilled; and after that he must be loosed a little season.' He suddenly gripped Mott's arm again with a surprising strength and glowered with fervour into the American's eyes. 'You *must* believe it! Today marks the end of Satan's thousand years and I intend to stop him – return him to his prison in hell for another thousand.'

Mott shifted uncomfortably on the hard wood of the pew. 'Well, if it's as you say, surely Old Nick will have some help with him. I doubt that you're going to be able to stand up to a full onslaught from that quarter.'

The words were meant kindly, to pacify the crazed

man. Falangi reacted to them by unexpectedly patting the arm and fixing Tom with an almost sly look. 'Oh yes, he will have help. Satan's own protector on earth will be called to the portal to guard it against me. His cacodemon has walked the earth these thousand years, taking the bodies of humans like a parasite and living, watching, waiting for the day. When the human he possesses dies, he simply moves to another, waiting in the darkness of the mind for the time when the summons comes and the host-body moves to the appointed place. Only then will the cacodemon reveal himself to stand ready to repel the forces of God. It has happened before, many times, and each time we have won. One day we may not, at which time Satan will emerge into the world and plunge it into the darkness of the damned.' He stopped talking and sat silently.

Mott studied the man and felt a wave of pity for him. 'This cacodemon you talk of, how do you know he's here?'

'His work has already been reported. The girl by the side of the road, the party of campers. They died at his hands. It left the host body, venturing forth to test its strength. The other deaths occurred because the cacodemon entered people's minds, causing them to carry out these wicked crimes – exploited flaws in their character.' He cast sad eyes around the church. 'Even the poor Father who lived here was susceptible to the influence of evil. God rest his soul.'

'So why don't you just stop the demon? Wouldn't that do the trick?'

Falangi laughed bitterly at the suggestion. 'I wish it were that easy! The cacodemon is only a guard.'

Mott felt the man was not playing games with him and he decided to challenge the story with an obvious question. 'You say this cacodemon is here in the village. Then you must know whose body it occupies.'

'I do. It occupies the body of an adult, orphaned at a young age.'

Mott felt the chill again. 'I'm an orphan,' he said flatly.

Falangi nodded. 'I know you are, Mr Mott, I know you are!'

'Your note said you wanted to talk to me about Doyle,' said Mott changing the subject.

'Your friend has become involved through his diligence to duty. Perhaps he is still alive, although I rather doubt he could survive a night in the company of the Devil.'

Mott grew increasingly irritated, demanding to know what information Falangi had of the lost man.

'Only that the night Doyle disappeared, I myself was in the cave, making preparations for the Trial. At one point I thought I was being followed, but after listening for a while, decided I was mistaken. On reflection, it might well have been him.'

'Then you must know roughly where he is. Why on earth haven't you told the authorities?'

Falangi looked saddened.. 'Impossible. The chamber must not be disturbed. Doyle must take his chances with the rest of us. There is nothing I can do for him now.'

Mott stood. 'I've heard enough, Father,' he said tightly. 'I suggest you start thinking about getting medical help – you're sick!' He turned without further word and walked briskly up the aisle, his footsteps reverberating uncomfortably through the cold church. As he reached the door he heard Falangi call out: 'You *are* involved, Mr Mott. You cannot escape from that involvement any more than I can!' Then Mott had stepped through the door into the deserted street, slamming the wooden door behind him.

Furious, he gunned the station wagon into action and sped along the road, half noticing the commotion outside the public house where two uniformed police officers were struggling with a blood-soaked man. The priest was mad, of that there could be no doubt, but there was the possibility that what he had said about Doyle could be true.

Mott had almost automatically discounted approaching Ambrose. If he was involved in the lunacy, there would be little satisfaction gained from that quarter. Seamus Flynn, on the other hand, might prove to be more profitable. The journalist had come to appreciate Flynn's commonsense approach to problems and his gentle, self-deprecating Irish humour. Perhaps Flynn would be able to see a way of checking the crazy priest's story.

His car flashed past their rented cottage and he thought briefly of the erotic nights he and Alana had spent there. He was still thinking of her when he arrived at Flynn's farmhouse with its untidy front yard.

Mott rang the doorbell and when he received no answer, moved around the side of the house to where another door led into the kitchen. At the table stood Flynn busy preparing a sandwich. He jumped as Mott rapped on the window pane.

'I rang the doorbell,' said Mott.

Flynn rolled his eyes towards the ceiling. 'I must be getting very deaf, I didn't hear you. Come on through to the parlour.'

Mott walked slightly ahead of the old man, entering what had once been a cosy room, reflecting the care and attention lavished on it by a woman who, knowing she would never have much in the way of worldly possessions, had cleaned and polished what she did have with love and pride.

Mott stood quite still, frozen by the unexpected sight. The room lay in chaos. The furniture had been smashed and stacked against the far wall. Already threadbare carpeting appeared to have been slashed and shredded, walls had been hacked allowing huge lumps of plaster to lie in dust-swirling clumps on the plain wooden floor.

A groan to his left made him turn and he gaped at the sight of the daughter standing with arms outstretched against a doorway, her fingers opening and closing, her face contorted in agony. As he watched, one sleeve of her novice's gown slipped a little and Mott saw the nails driven through her slender wrist into the wooden door frame. His eyes dropped to the floor and he saw with revulsion, similar nailing through alabaster white ankles. Flynn had crucified his own daughter!

He turned to face the old man, aware of the rasping breath and terrible smell now penetrating the small living room. As he did so, a deep voice sounded from the man's throat, coming in hacking, foul tones which seemed to make the air still, as though it were tensing for an even worse outrage.

'The whore needs to learn the meaning of her Christ's suffering if she is to serve him,' the voice said slyly, 'but she only has to swear allegiance to the All Highest and she can be saved.'

Mott howled in fury and struck out, landing the blow squarely on Flynn's cheek. He staggered backwards and then lunged forward, leaping on Mott's back to clasp incredibly strong hands around his throat. Tom tried to shake the man off but he felt legs entwined around his waist, gripping with unyielding intensity.

Sensing the nearness of the wall behind him, Tom stepped backwards sharply and heard the gratifying howl of pain from Flynn's lips as his spine hit the wall. Mott immediately repeated the action with as much strength as he could muster. Flynn's back once again slammed into the wall and Mott felt the grip relax slightly. The journalist threw himself into a violent rocking motion which sent Seamus flying from his back to lie, momentarily winded, on the floor.

With scarcely a glance at his fallen assailant, he crossed quickly to the girl, took up the claw hammer lying near her right foot and prepared to remove the nail from her left wrist. He knew he would need something to wedge under the hammer head if he were to avoid causing her more pain than was necessary. He removed a shoe, placing it alongside her wrist and gently slipped the claw under the nail head.

As pressure was applied she opened her eyes to stare at him with their deep, haunting sorrow. Then her features changed to those of intense fear and he whirled about in time to see Flynn advancing on him with raised hand, in which glinted a strong butcher's knife, used for gutting the rabbits Flynn poached from nearby estates.

Mott ducked as the blade descended and grappled for the outstretched arm. Again he felt Flynn's superhuman strength as the weapon was forced, ever closer, towards his face. Mott glared into the snarling face and incredibly bright eyes.

Despite his own strength, Tom knew he would lose the fight as his own grip weakened and Flynn, almost casually, applied yet more power to his arm.

And then, just when all seemed lost, Flynn's expression softened. The brightness in his eyes seemed to dim and they transmitted uncertainty. Mott felt the arm weaken and seized his chance, pushing against the Irishman with all his strength, propelling him across the room. Flynn stumbled and Mott overbalanced and catapulted forward to land on top of him, driving the knife deep into Flynn's chest with the weight of his body.

As Mott's head smashed into the gleaming brass fire surround and he began to lose consciousness, he heard Flynn's death-rattle. Blackness enveloped his mind while distantly, he heard the sound of the novice's mumbled prayers.

The persistent ringing reached him and eventually ceased. He slipped gratefully back into sleep and then was vaguely aware of being hauled to his feet and frog-marched to a source of fresh air. Someone was slapping his face. Reluctantly, he opened his eyes to see the face of a young man looking with concern into his own.

'Are you all right, mister?'

Mott ran a hand to his brow and found the open wound, running deep and broad across his forehead. There was blood on his fingertips. It was as though the hand belonged to someone else as he examined it dispassionately. He felt weak, displaced, unable to understand fully what had taken place. Fleetingly, at first, the memory started to filter back.

'Are you all right?' repeated the voice hollowly. Mott nodded. He wasn't really but he didn't feel much like talking.

'What in the blue Jasus has been going on here?' asked the voice.

'Old man went mad,' muttered Mott, suddenly aware he was standing with the officer in the doorway of the kitchen, pleased his vision wasn't impaired as he had at first suspected. It was dark outside! He groaned at the thought of the last vital footage they were supposed to get; of the soundman sent to replace Doyle waiting with Alana on the windy hill; of the crazed Flynn now unable to lead his pathetic procession of modern-day Druids, incanting modern rituals in ridiculous parody of the ancients. In a flash Mott decided it didn't matter anymore. Harman could go screw himself!

'What time is it?' he asked, the effort of speaking sending shock waves through his skull.

'Half-past ten. We've been looking for you for hours. One of the lads had been here earlier but when he didn't get an answer . . .' the rest of the sentence trailed away. 'Anyway, I came round to see Christine to say goodbye. She was to leave for the convent tomorrow.'

'Christine? . . . oh, the girl! How is she?'

The officer looked angrily away. 'Dead! So is her mother upstairs. Look, what *did* happen?'

'I told you, the old man went crazy!'

'And he knocked out a big lad like you?' he snapped back in disbelief.

'No, I managed that on my own. Look, call Ambrose on your radio and tell him what's happening here will you?'

'I already have. My instructions are to take you to him. We've been searching for you because your Miss Kennedy has gone missing. She went into the tunnel system to look for the other one and hasn't been seen since. Colonel Ambrose says that there is nothing more that can be done here.' The words came out with enormous bitterness that Christine's death could mean so little. He had loved the girl and up to that night had hoped to change her mind about taking the veil.

Mott allowed himself to be steered towards the police car where he slumped without further words into the back seat.

The car raced through the darkened village and then turned left at the crossroads before swinging onto the track which would take them to the brow of the hill. The journey was a blur to Mott, who witnessed the passing terrain as though he were somehow divorced from his body, looking down at the speeding police vehicle from just outside, yet speeding along within it, intent on watching the rest of Mott's personal nightmare.

All too soon for Tom, the car slowed and the rear door opened. Tom was helped out, still confused. He mumbled thanks to the young officer who had found him at Flynn's house and lifted his head with painful effort.

He had expected the brow of the hill to be a hive of activity, rescue vehicles and men milling around, waiting for news of the missing couple, or preparing to enter the cave to conduct yet more searches of the system far below his feet. Instead, he saw only the single bent figure of the priest, dressed in black with a large cross hanging about his neck. A noise behind him made him glance over his shoulder and he saw the police car receding down the hill. They were alone!

'What's going on, Falangi?'

'Miss Kennedy is in the cave!' replied the priest, jerking a thumb over his shoulder, towards the cave mouth. 'I knew you'd be concerned!'

Mott looked around. 'Sure, I am!'

Falangi hobbled forward. 'There is no time, we must hurry. I know where she is. Are you coming?' He turned and walked quickly towards the cave entrance, stooping at a rock to retrieve his leather bag from the ground. With only one glance back towards Mott, Falangi ducked into the opening and Mott saw the shaft of light from his torch reflecting outward and then slowly dim, as the priest moved into the tunnel.

Tom stood alone for several seconds, wondering what he should do. If Alana were in danger . . . His mind made up, he moved to the entrance and slid his large frame through, moving down the tunnel towards the glow of Falangi's torch.

Above ground, the heavens opened with a clamorous

peal of thunder which rolled on and on across the valley, causing the people of Craghan to lock their doors and making them wonder what strange forces were abroad this night of Samhain.

CHAPTER THIRTEEN

Falangi led the way unerringly to the large cavern where earlier Flynn's search party had called off the attempts to locate Doyle. Surprisingly, the line, so carefully strung along the complex by Flynn, was no longer in evidence. Falangi explained to Mott that the army had removed it after abandoning their full-scale search operation. They couldn't run the risk of youngsters from the village following the string and then inadvertently getting lost by wandering away from the route.

Once inside the main cavern, Falangi had quickly got his bearings and led Tom on and into a second, more tortuous system. Twisting and turning, Falangi exuded all the confidence needed to prevent unnecessary questioning from the American, who still felt the effects of his concussion and hardly felt talkative. It was only when they had walked down this last, narrow tunnel and were faced by a solid wall of granite that Mott's cynicism returned. The priest did not, after all, know where Alana was.

His guide placed his small leather bag on the floor and quickly unfastened it. By the light of the powerful torch he withdrew a small phial of clear liquid and a dark brown leather-bound book with a large, gold clasp holding the pages together. Falangi carefully removed the glass stopper from the bottle and sprinkled the contents against the wall, murmuring a blessing as he did so. Then, he opened the book and began mumbling in a language unfamiliar to Mott. It might have been Greek but he couldn't be sure. Mott started to speak, to ask Falangi what he was doing, but the old man waved an impatient hand at him to be still.

At length, he closed the *Book of the Preparation for the Trial* and repacked it into the bag, along with the phial and stepped back beside Mott. 'You are about to see something not seen by human eyes for many hundreds of years, Thomas. When we are inside please do exactly what I tell you to. Do not believe anything you see and listen only to my instructions. Is that perfectly clear?'

Mott looked through the swirling mist at the priest. 'Inside? Inside where?'

Falangi waved the torch, its beam bouncing off the wall ahead. 'In there. Watch!'

As he spoke, the air about them became charged with an unseen energy and Mott felt the hair on the back of his neck prickle and the skin stretch tighter over his bones. Ahead of them, he could discern ripples in the air as though some mysterious form of heat was rising. Shifting and displacing, the waves merged and formed a curtain so solid it blocked out all sight of the wall itself.

And then the waves receded and Mott let out an involuntary gasp when he saw the archway which had appeared in the wall. Beyond it a soft blue light was shining from some distance away. He turned to Falangi, an unspoken question in his eyes. 'Remember, Thomas,' said the priest, as he stepped through the archway, 'do only what I tell you and believe nothing. Nothing whatever.'

As they walked forward, Mott noticed the foulness of the air and the swirling yellow mist that hung cloyingly close to the ground, billowing about their ankles.

An icy chill passed through Mott's body, although the palms of his hands were clammy. There was no doubting the transmogrification of the wall; nor this strange entrance to . . . to what? He began to feel detached from the events surrounding him. It was as though he was conscious of leaving his body, watching himself follow the priest. He assumed the sulphuric fumes were affecting him and was about to call out to Falangi when suddenly, around a corner, he caught sight of Alana. She was still, her back to them, staring towards a huge opening in the stone wall from which emanated the strange blue light.

'Alana!' he shouted and felt the restraining hand on his arm.

'She can't hear you. Alana is catatonic at this point. Don't go near or disturb her and perhaps we shall at least save her.'

Mott whirled on the man. 'All right you crazy bastard,' he stormed, 'what the hell is going on? What have you done to her?'

Falangi walked towards the girl and placed his bag on the ground to her left before turning to face Tom. '*I* have done nothing to her. As to what is going on, surely you can see for yourself? Look around! In heaven's name look around you!'

Mott cast his eyes around the cave, taking in the macabre setting. Like the entrance of the cave, it appeared to have been carved out of the rock with rudimentary tools. Crude carvings of figures and symbols were chiselled haphazardly into the stone, testament, perhaps, to some sinister ritual. The dimensions of the cave were staggering. Tom estimated the distance between him and the far wall to be approximately eighty feet with the roof of the cave probably in excess of forty feet high.

Near to where Falangi now stood, roughly in the centre, were several dozen white shapes carefully positioned on the ground. Tom recognised the rough shape of a large pentacle, with its carefully prepared symbols of fire, earth, water, life and death. In the centre of the pentacle lay three small bones.

Falangi pointed with a shaking finger towards the source of the blue light and Mott turned his attention to the great slabs of stone which formed the frame of the entrance and the massive lintel resting across the top. Inscriptions were carved into the stone and Tom recognised the Greek, Latin, Gaelic and uncial lettering carved at different periods in the earth's history. And then his eyes came to rest on a crumpled body lying on its back at the very edge of the portal. Only by the clothes did he know it to be the body of his soundman. Doyle's hair was now completely grey, matching the ashen face, and dull, lifeless eyes bulged from their sockets. His face still registered a look of pure terror, the last emotion he had ever felt. A deep wound in his chest revealed that the once pulsating heart had been ripped out violently from its sanctuary.

Mott turned slowly to Falangi. For the first time in his life he knew what it was to be afraid.

'That is the portal through which the Devil will attempt to enter this world,' said the priest, the tiredness evident in his voice. 'I told you I would explain the whole story, my son, and that time has now come. Shortly, Satan will attempt that which he has been prevented from doing since the dawn of time – prevented for the last two thousand years by my Church on each of the two occasions when he tried to claim the world as his. Before Christianity it was the responsibility of the Druidic priests; before them, the responsibility of pagan priests. Before them, it was the duty of the Guardian alone to keep this place secure – this and others scattered throughout our world.

'Every thousand years he is strong enough to throw off the shackles which bind him. Every thousand years we have prevented him and will continue to do so for each subsequent thousand years. For if we fail to, our punishment will be to wallow in the darkness, forgotten souls condemned to everlasting damnation.

'I was chosen to be one of the Guardians many years ago and I have spent my life and strength in preparing for this moment. The only weapon which can stop me from preventing Satan's return is his own earthly protector. The cacodemon who has brought such terror to the village above us.'

Mott had recovered his composure by now and his professional scepticism had returned. 'Ah yes, your cacodemon! You told me about that in the church. If you expect me . . .'

Falangi was suddenly furious. 'Look, do you not see the awful truth? Can you not see that light which comes from Hell itself? Alana, standing possessed? Can you not see these things? Doesn't the sight of the actual portal fill you with dread; doesn't it recall memories in you?'

Mott struggled to hold on to reality. He couldn't allow his mind to be manipulated and in panic, shouted back at the priest, 'I see a crazy old man, who can perform a pretty good party trick with a wall and a man who's been murdered! I can see you standing in a black magic circle and Alana drugged! That's what I can see. Nothing else!'

Falangi ran his bony right hand through thick white hair and looked about him. 'Thomas, this circle is the only protection I have and even this will probably not be enough to save me. The pentagram is formed by pieces of the Eucharist and these bones are three of St Peter's given to me by the Pope. They must be thrown into the portal at the appointed time to close it off once again, sealing Satan inside for another thousand years. The cacodemon must prevent me from my task. That is his only function . . . to stop me from hurtling his master back into the pit.'

'This cacodemon is the one possessing a human body?' asked Tom in a voice in which there was just a trace of fear.

At that moment Alana groaned slightly and snapped her head towards them, 'Tom, oh Tom, what's happening?'

Mott moved forward to help her. Falangi raised a hand quickly and cried out fearfully. 'STOP, you must *not* go near her!'

'Why not?' the journalist shouted back.

'Tom, I believe you thought I meant you when I said the demon had taken the body of an orphan. But it's not in you. This, of course, could never be. It's Alana! The cacodemon lives in Alana's mind!'

Mott looked disbelievingly at the calm priest and then across to the beautiful girl, who still stood near to the portal as though rooted to the spot. He began to laugh, softly at first, and then louder. 'You really are crazy, you know.'

'Tom, what's he saying? Help me, I can't move!'

The priest stepped from his protective circle and gripped Mott's arm tightly. 'Listen to me, Tom. Listen hard. She is trying to trick you into going closer before your full strength comes. She is possessed.

'I first knew of her when she was at an orphanage in New York. One evening she took a babysitting assignment over the state line in New Jersey. Tom, she murdered her charge! She roasted it in the oven!'

Tom was silent for a moment, horrified by the story. Then quite suddenly, he realised this aged priest must be telling the truth. Honesty shone from his care-worn eyes like a beacon; no deception could be concealed in their depths. 'Go on,' he finally murmured, his mouth dry.

'She was sent to a state hospital for a while, but

eventually released into her aunt's care. The aunt returned with the girl to Ireland. Alana would have been about eighteen at the time and had no memory of the terrible crime she had committed. How could she have when it was the demon who perpetrated it? If we are to save her, do *not* go near and ignore anything she might say to you until the strength comes. And it will come!'

Tom studied the weathered face. 'What strength? What are you talking about?'

A deep rumble sounded from the portal accompanied by an intense red light, blinding them momentarily. Falangi stepped quickly back into his circle. At the same time, Alana began a low chuckling which rose higher and deeper before erupting with ear-shattering force around their heads.

'Tom, your presence here has been designed. Without your help in protecting me, Satan will win. *Remember who you are!* Remember the times before when you have stood with other priests in other places and fought the cacodemon. Remember, Tom, remember you are the Eternal One – *you* are Gilgamesh!'

At the very utterance of the name a scream of fury erupted from Alana's throat and Tom swung around to face the girl. The lines of her mouth were contorted and a foulness poured from it to ooze onto the floor at her feet. Then the light intensified and Alana's body collapsed to the floor and in her place stood the evil cacodemon, hatred radiating from its body, its slanted eyes darting from the priest to Tom.

It towered above them, a colossus of predatory evil and corruption. Large pointed ears jutted from a hard, scaly head which seemed to be cleft in two by a solid ridge of bone, running from the forehead across the skull to meet the spinal cord. Its nose, set flat against a distorted face, rose and fell as it breathed and large fangs showed clearly in its mouth. And the cat-like eyes darted around the cavern watching its master's enemies, preparing for action.

Naked, one claw fondled its massive organ as though seeking a warm orifice to thrust into. It hissed and spat at Falangi before turning to guide all its hate towards the one who so often had been sent to help thwart the plans of the Master. Crouching slightly, it began to advance.

Tom stepped back at the hideous sight and only faintly heard the priest calling him to remember. And then the memory of it all began to filter back into his mind. The primeval swamps, with the small circle of warriors gathered fearfully, casting anxious glances into the unfriendly jungle. And there to give them his support was the tall man with raven-black hair and bright eyes which radiated hope. And then later a different grouping in a different place, but in the centre this same man repelling the evil that came through the night on this special day. White-hooded priests now stood at a stone circle and again he was there to stop the evil gaining a foothold on this fragile world peopled by fragile souls. He was needed, had been needed, throughout this world's tortured history.

He was needed now!

Falangi breathed a little easier as Tom Mott stopped his backward retreat, and smiled in gratitude as he watched the already tall figure grow in stature, a brilliance in his eyes radiating the strength of Christ's Champion.

The demon hesitated on seeing his adversary stop and from its mouth came a low grumbling.

'Ehieh,

'Iod,

'Tetragrammaton Elohim,

'El,

'Elohim Gibor,

'Eloah V a-Daath.'

'He's calling out the nine divinities of hell to send forth

the minions to aid him. Destroy him quickly, Eternal One!' screamed Falangi.

The demon heard the priest and stopped his incantation. It snarled at Falangi and shuffled forward. A cloven hoof touched a small piece of communion wafer and, shrieking, it fell back as though its foot had touched acid.

Growling, it resumed:

'El Adonai Tzaboath,

'Elohim Tzaboath,

'Shaddai.'

Instantly, a hurricane of wind filled the cavern, driving Falangi tottering almost to the very edge of the circle and into the arms of the waiting horror. Mott stepped forward, impervious to the lashing maelstrom, and embraced the cacodemon.

Taloned fingers lashed at his face in an attempt to escape from the powerful grasp of the Eternal One. Again and again the talons raked the face, gouging and tearing. Fangs sank into warm flesh and tore at the muscular frame, but Mott felt no pain as the Eternal One took control.

Falangi watched the battle between Heaven and Hell's champions move to and fro across the cave floor, first the demon gaining an advantage and then Gilgamesh. Falangi knew the portal had been opened with the completion of the demon's utterances and even now he could feel the threatening approach of Satan himself. Time was now disjointed and as long as the portal remained open, Satan could cross and all would be lost.

The priest looked down at the ground and saw that his protective circle had been destroyed, the holy wafers scattered about the floor like leaves on an autumn day. The three bones remained in place, untouched by the winds from Hell. He scooped them up and edged around the wall, fearful that the demon would sense what he was doing and make a last lunge to stop him. He had to arrive at the portal before the sight of Satan froze him into inaction; had to cast the holy relics of the founder of the Church into the opening at just the correct time, at the point where time was most meaningless.

The cacodemon was clasped to Gilgamesh/Mott in an obscene embrace as Falangi reached the portal. He quoted passages from the *Book of the Preparation for the Trial*, exhorting God to protect him and aid him. He drew back his arm to hurl St Peter's bones into the pit and heard the howl of rage and fury from the demon.

He closed his eyes as he heard the demon break loose from his captor and race across the cave to stop him. Even as the bones left his hand he opened his eyes for a brief moment to see the face of the Dark One approaching out of the blackness of the foul pit. And then the demon slammed into his unguarded back, catapaulting them both, as one, into the yawning mouth of the portal—

A tortured howl rose from the pit and the red light faded away. It was all over. The portal had been resealed.

The spirit of Gilgamesh rose sorrowfully from Mott's body and looked down on the scene at those who had died to complete the Trial. The spirit looked at the mutilated body of Doyle and then of Alana, her sensuousness extinguished forever. And at the torn, shredded body of the man called Tom Mott. He had served well enough. But the time had come to seek another host and then another and another until the Trial came again.

He looked fleetingly towards the portal through which Father Falangi had been propelled and knew God would be unable to save him from that place. The good priest would have understood and accepted it.

And then the spirit that had lived as Mott, in Mott,

rose on through the granite and the sandstone, through the earth and grass into the pure night air, which it did not breathe, had no need to breathe. The Eternal One looked up at the bright, twinkling stars flashing their message of hope in the clear morning sky . . .

. . . and he would return!

EPILOGUE

Monsignor Molinari replaced the French provincial-style telephone into its cradle with slow deliberation and turned to his visitor. 'His Holiness will see us in ten minutes, Colonel. Perhaps you would care to finish your story while we wait?'

Ambrose drained the last of the bitter Italian coffee and carefully placed the bone china cup and saucer on the highly-polished side table, sifting his thoughts as he did so to pick up the threads of their interrupted conversation. He fingered the black patch over his damaged eye and recalled the violent attack upon him by the Garda officer in the police station cell which had blinded him in that eye. Patrick would never learn of the evil which had possessed him. Better he live the rest of his life in confusion, believing the story that he had blacked out and fallen, damaging his own sight in the process. Although Patrick had accepted the tale, Ambrose knew that the officer struggled to recall the events of that afternoon, struggled for a memory that was just out of reach. For his own sanity it was better. As it was for the many people in Craghan who would never learn the truth behind the terrible events which had befallen their once happy village.

The security chief nodded towards the package lying on the corner of Molinari's ornate desk. 'There is little else to add. After I left Father Falangi and Mott in the church I went directly to the cottage and retrieved the document and its case from Mott's bedroom. I took it straight to Dublin and locked it in my office safe as Falangi had requested. Then I immediately returned to Craghan and waited until dawn – again, as instructed by Father Falangi.'

Ambrose fell silent for a moment and Molinari waited patiently, recognising that the man needed time to compose himself as his ghastly memories were turned into words. Ambrose recalled leaving the police station just as the cold fingers of dawn crept over the surrounding hillside and driving alone up the narrow track to the Cave of Cruachu.

'When I got to the cave entrance it was just after dawn,' he said, brushing at a speck of dust on his trouser leg. 'At first, I could see no sign of anyone. There had been a fall of rock at the entrance which now makes entry totally impossible. I looked around the area and discovered the body of Mott. Only his!

'Monsignor, I don't fully understand what had happened but Falangi told me that I could expect to find Mott's body on the hillside and that it was quite possible we would find no trace of the others. He also told me something else which I hadn't believed until I saw Mott's body . . .'

Molinari leaned forward in his chair as the officer paused in his attempt to speak of the events. He added helpfully: 'Father Falangi told you that you would find Mr Mott's body but the skin would be flayed from it, is that correct?'

Ambrose nodded dully. 'Yes. I didn't recognise him for some time. The body was wet from the seeping body fluid covering the corpse. The epidermis itself trailed behind the body, attached only at the ankles. God, it was a horrible sight.'

Molinari sat patiently as the man fought to regain his

composure. 'And so you severed the remaining pieces of skin from the ankles and hid them in your car. Is that right?'

Colonel Ambrose swallowed hard and raised his head. 'Yes. Then I returned to the police station and called for assistance to make a full search of the area. Nothing else was found. It will take several weeks to clear away the rock fall and by then anybody trapped in the cave will be dead. Monsignor, events have happened to me and around me that I just do not understand! Father Falangi told me to do and expect certain things. He had informed me that if I hadn't heard from him by the end of the day to contact you and you would explain as much as you could. I'd appreciate that explanation now. Quite frankly I feel as though I'm in danger of losing my mind!'

Molinari sighed, rose from the desk and crossed to the window. A sunbeam shone through the window bathing him in its warmth, but despite this he still felt cold, unable to shake off the all-encroaching numbness. It had started to take hold after they had informed him of the discovery in the Catacombs of his friend Cardinal Barretta, torn apart by some unspeakable force. How many more must die over the years before the war could finally be won?

He shivered suddenly and crossed to the couch to sit beside Ambrose. 'I agree, you deserve an explanation, Colonel.

'Many years ago, Father Falangi worked at an orphanage in New York. He was a young, concerned priest who was marked for great things in the Church's hierarchy. However, the hand of fate intervened and cast Falangi onto another, more important path.

'One of the orphans, a girl called Caroline Michaels,

committed a most terrible crime while she baby-sat for a young couple. Many of the senior girls did such assignments for the extra pocket money and Caroline was one of the most trusted of all the teenagers. She murdered the baby!

'Father Falangi met with the child many times afterwards while she was in a state hospital, and he formed the opinion that she had been possessed at the time she had committed the deed for she had no recollection afterwards of having harmed the child. He concluded therefore that the cacodemon lay dormant in her subconscious mind. He reported his findings to his bishop and eventually the Papal office was apprised of the case. We ordered a close watch to be kept on the girl, knowing that it was this type of person who would be harbouring Lucifer's earthly protector. Naturally, the Church at that time was keeping watch on a great many other such cases.'

'Why? Why at that time?'

Molinari looked levelly back at the Colonel. 'Because we knew that the time for Satan to make his bid for the souls of mankind was very near. We have watched and waited since the end of the last war for a sign, hoping we would be able to find the earthly body that the cacodemon had possessed in order that we could plot its progress and be in the correct place at the appointed time.'

'Why not just wait at the cave if you knew it would figure so prominently?'

A short, bitter laugh emanated from the Monsignor's throat. 'Would that it were that easy, Colonel! There are many such portals through which Satan could enter this world. Equally, the Prince of Darkness is clever and many times he tried to trick us to the wrong location. It was only two years ago that we knew we had found the right area, but even then we didn't know for sure where the exact location of the portal was.'

'Two years ago?' murmured Ambrose. 'That incident at the Abbey,' he said suddenly, 'was that all a part of it?'

'Yes. His Holiness went to the Abbey to start Father Falangi on his mission. It could have been a priest in any one of the numerous countries that the Pope visited that year, who sat waiting, ready to answer the call. But it was Father Falangi who finally had to finish what started so many years previously in his own orphanage.' He sounded sad at the thought and Ambrose began to wonder if the truth was worse than not knowing.

'But there wasn't anyone called Caroline Michaels involved,' he quickly said.

'No, you knew her as Alana Kennedy. You see after her crime she was committed to a state mental hospital. Her age precluded a prison term. After several years she was released into the care of an aunt who then left America to return to her native Ireland. Her name was Kennedy. The aunt also changed the girl's christian name to ensure new friends and neighbours wouldn't discover who she had been. Bear in mind, Colonel, Alana had no memory of the deed. She was a vessel carrying a creature. Nothing more. Father Falangi had hoped to lure her into St Bernadette's in order to drive out the cacodemon. Unfortunately in its cunning the demon detoured her away from the village.'

Molinari leaned across the couch and patted the man's arm. 'We haven't the time to tell you the entire history of the man within the man, Colonel, but suffice it to say that he was a very important part of the Trial. As the Devil has an earthly protector, so does Christ. It took us a long time to isolate Mott as that Champion; we had been watching many men whose lives seemed to be exceptionally hazardous and who nevertheless survived unscathed. Through the vigilance of our churchmen it became clear that Mott was the only possible Gilgamesh, as Christ's protector, the Eternal One, is called. All his life the hordes of the Devil have tried to place Mott into mortal danger and equally he has been protected all through his troubled time on this earth by the forces of the one God,' Molinari sighed resignedly. 'I suppose it sounds too much, too incredible, but I assure you that the Trial had to be accepted and the loss of life unavoidable. It will happen again, of that there can be no doubt. Even now the forces of darkness muster themselves to seek another way through. Perhaps they will not wait another thousand years. Who knows?'

Abruptly, Molinari stood and moved towards the desk to slip the package into a drawer before locking it with a slender key. He slipped the key into a hidden pocket in his clothing and turned back to Ambrose as the Colonel asked in a questioning tone: 'But that manuscript and the . . . skin . . . how do they fit in?'

Molinari looked down at the drawer. 'The skin of Tom Mott will be used to bind another folder while another portion will be used to contain a message that will be read by another generation. The manuscript and folder you brought back to me is the skin of a man who perished in a similar way a thousand years ago – that folder will be placed, along with others of its kind in a special place to mark the progress of the ages, the progress of each Trial.'

Ambrose was horrified at this news and his face expressed the disgust which he felt. 'That's barbaric, Monsignor. I never thought I would hear this sort of thing from . . .'

'From the Catholic Church? Colonel, there are many things we do which would cause alarm if they were to be known. But there are many things which must be done to ensure the continuance of this imperfect world with its imperfect souls.'

Ambrose couldn't accept the answer and pressed for another to his original question. But what's it *used* for?'

Molinari chuckled slightly, wearily. 'A stage-prop, really. Nothing more. Oh, the message is of great importance, but in reality it is a stage prop used in the same way as a fake library and an Arab who simply did as we asked. Thomas Mott became intrigued by it, as we hoped he would. Its disappearance in Rome helped ensure he would go to Ireland, while its reappearance ensured he would remain where he was until the end of the Trial.'

'Fake library? Arab? I don't understand!'

'It doesn't matter, Colonel. Believe me, it doesn't matter.'

Ambrose stood and faced the churchman. 'And you say that it will all happen again – all this has really been for nothing!'

A light buzzer sounded once from the intercom box on the desk and Molinari indicated they should walk towards the door by the ornate fireplace. 'Yes, one day Lucifer will try again. He is a devious master, constantly ingratiating himself in the minds of men, securing new footholds in the most unlikely of places. Oh yes, one day, unless the Church or our successors remain vigilant, he will try again. Perhaps it is all for nothing. Perhaps we should allow him in, bow to the inevitable. But I think the souls of mankind are worth fighting for, don't you, Colonel Ambrose?'

He turned the brass handle on the door and allowed

Ambrose to walk through into the Pope's private library. Pope John Paul II rose from his couch as Ambrose entered and greeted his guest.

Monsignor Molinari stepped inside the room and turned to pull the door shut behind him. As he did so, he caught sight of his reflection in the full-length mirror on the far wall of his own office, behind the couch. For a brief moment a bright light shone from the dark eyes and the mirrored image smiled a tight, cruel smile.

'*And I too will return*,' said the voice in his mind as Molinari stepped into the room, closing the door behind him.

THE FURY

John Farris

Michael and Sandra are 14 years old. They were born with the power to speak without speech . . . And to kill without contact.

They are:

THE FURY

'Horrifying, terrifying chiller . . . a sexy, violent, sadistic, psychic novel that's filled with skulduggery, witchcraft, chases and all manner of spooky, unsavoury stuff'.
Publishers Weekly

'An absolutely terrifying read'
Paul E. Erdman, author of 'The Crash of '79'

The most frightening novel of supernatural terror since SALEM'S LOT and THE OMEN.

Fiction
0 8600 7566 4

DAMIEN : OMEN 2

Joseph Howard

The nerve-shattering sequel to *The Omen*, the super-selling shocker of supernatural evil.
An ancient mural is discovered amidst the suffocating dusts of the Jordan Valley - Yigael's Satan, a portrait older than time, giving incontestable proof that the Devil lives in Damien Thorn.

Robert Thorn saw Satan in his son, and died violently. Seven years later, Damien has been adopted by Richard Thorn, head of an international industrial empire. The boy is clearly intended to become his uncle's heir, a position of awsome potential power for good – or evil. And gradually those around him begin to realise the terrible truth . . .

* Also available: *The Omen* by David Seltzer